DATE DUE			

NOT WITHOUT PARABLES

NOT WITHOUT PARABLES

Stories of Yesterday, Today and Eternity

248.

Doff

Catherine de Hueck Doherty

Ave Maria Press
Notre Dame, Indiana 46556

Library of Congress Catalog Card Number: 76-50488
International Standard Book Number: 0-87793-126-7 (Cloth)
0-87793-127-5 (Paper)

art credits: Janet Lukos
Patti Birdsong
Tom Hojnacki

To my son George

Contents

Introduction

When I was a child my mother and father taught me by stories. Because I had traveled much during my childhood, these stories were in many languages, and many of them were taken from the folklore of the pilgrims and peasants. Yes, I have come from a country and a generation that *listened*— an oral generation, in many ways—that transmitted its lore, history and traditions through stories and parables.

Strange to say, I have found that in this sophisticated, technological generation of Canada and the United States, the hearts of people also yearn for stories, for explanations of things wrapped up in symbols which are somewhat mysterious, yet simple. From the very beginning of our Madonna House Apostolate I have used stories, and they have been understood and loved by young and old alike. I still continue to speak in stories. They come naturally to me. The Russians, like the Irish, the Arabs and many other peoples, are natural storytellers.

Collected in this book are some of the stories that were told to me, some I have made up myself, and some are based on incidents that have happened to us. The stories in Part III, the "How Stories" as they are known around Madonna House, are obviously from my own imagination. The "Blue Door Stories" are actual happenings, retold as well as I can remember them. Most of them were written many years ago, much closer to the actual events.

The only stories that do not fit into a neat category are

9

the "Pilgrim Stories." They are recounted to you as well as I can remember them as told to me. Did they "actually happen"? Again, I can only say that this is how they were told to me. They flow from the lives and adventures of people pilgrimaging around Russia in search of God. Were they dreams? Were they the fruit of fertile imaginations? Were they visions due to excessive fastings and prayers and vigils? Or were they true visitations from God and from our Lady? (These are truly "Western" questions!) The stories are true because their message is true. The rest must be left to the heart of each reader.

Over the years I have written many books (most recently, *Poustinia* and *The Gospel Without Compromise**) in an attempt to share my understanding of the gospel with others. Stories are simply another way of doing this. Jesus often spoke in story form. How we love stories! Why are they so powerful in helping us understand and remember deep truths about life? Isn't it because stories are closer to life than mere ideas? Jesus knew this. He, the Master Teacher, told the most beautiful and the most unforgettable stories in the history of the world. They are so deep that they are now woven into the very fiber of our hearts and minds.

I hope that the stories which follow will also help to bring home to your hearts the deep truths of the gospel.

Catherine de Hueck Doherty
Madonna House
Combermere, Ontario

*Ave Maria Press

"In all this teaching to the crowds Jesus spoke in parables; in fact he never spoke to them without a parable." (Mt 13:34)

I

Stories of Yesterday

The Pilgrims

Some of the wonderful experiences I had as a child are connected with the stories of the holy pilgrims who passed through the Russia of old on their way to and from shrines. My mother and father welcomed these men and women very hospitably when, as was the pilgrims' custom, they knocked on our door and asked for food and shelter for the night. Like all the homes in Russia, ours was open to travelers. It was a blessing to harbor these saintly people. Walking across country, they had observed and remembered much.

Russian pilgrimages have become the fashion these days. One is not "in" unless he has read *The Way of the Pilgrim*. Salinger even mentioned it a few years ago in one of his novels.

The Way of the Pilgrim is a good book, a profound book. It is the story of an ordinary peasant who pilgrims across Holy Russia visiting various shrines. In reality, it is his *soul* that pilgrims toward the Absolute. Yes, it is a wonderful book. I have read it in my native language, Russian, and in French and English.

Nevertheless, I do not consider myself privileged because I have read the book, but because I have met pilgrims like the one described in the book. In fact, I have been such a pilgrim myself.

My mother and I have gone on long pilgrimages, barefooted, with no provisions other than a loaf of rye bread, a pinch of salt, a gourd of water and a prayer in our hearts. As for shelter in the evenings, and food when our own ran out, well, we became beggars like all the others.

In these ecumenical times, with the tremendous interest there is presently in the Eastern Church and Eastern spirituality, one way I can help foster this interest is to recall the stories I heard in my childhood. The constant stream of pilgrims who came to our house were simple men and women who spoke, of course, in symbols about their own experiences with God, with our Lady and with the saints. Always, hardly realizing it themselves, they revealed that soul of Russia that puzzles so many people in the West. Understanding is the key to reunion. Unless the West understands the East, and vice versa, the possibility of reunion will remain remote.

The very fact of the pilgrim's existence, even during the First World War and after (I understand such pilgrims still exist in Russia because the Communists were unable to stop their sacred journeys), is peculiar to the Russian soul. The notion of pilgrimage is deeply ingrained in the consciousness of the people. Russians are deeply aware of the fact that all men are really exiles from heaven, and that all of life is a pilgrimage. But they are also deeply aware of the fact that they can participate in the atoning sacrifice of Christ by the practice of their faith, and by the spiritual and corporal works of mercy, by mortification, penance, silence and prayer.

Pilgrimages combine many of these features. Definitely, they are undertaken with a spirit of atonement and prayer, atonement for one's own sins and then for the sins of mankind. The sense of the Mystical Body of Christ is also very strong in the Russian soul. One can never pray only for oneself. *One should always pray for the whole world.*

Thus, pilgrimages were works of atonement and prayer. They were also works of penance and mortification. No pilgrim in Russia ever took any money along on his journey. As for clothes, in the warm months they wore a linen shirt, tied in the middle with a string. For food they took, as I've mentioned in reference to my mother and myself, a gourd of water, a loaf of rye bread and a pinch of salt. They broke their fast twice a day, with the bread and the water. If they walked in a group, they walked in single file, one after the other, reciting litanies from time to time, chanting hymns— but mostly they walked in silent recollection. At eventide they came to villages and begged for food and shelter from the villagers. Since one of my intentions is ecumenical, perhaps it would be helpful to elaborate a bit on the different approach to fasting in the East and the West.

In regard to Lenten fasts and the many fasts and abstinences for the vigils of great feasts, the main idea was that older people should fast more than the younger ones. In the days of old, the Russians used to keep a "black fast" during Lent and Advent, during the two weeks preceding the feasts of Peter and Paul, and on some vigils before the feasts of our Lady.

A black fast (which I understand was also kept in places like Ireland) consisted of not eating meat, milk, or any milk products such as cheese or butter. No eggs were allowed either. Vegetable oil was used for cooking. The diet consisted mostly of boiled vegetables. There was no sugar. Honey was substituted instead, being a biblical sweetener made by the work of virgin bees.

Meat was allowed only on Sunday, and fish on Mondays, Tuesdays and Thursdays. Wednesday, in atonement for Judas' betrayal, was a day of fast and abstinence throughout the whole year. So was Friday, the day of Christ's crucifixion, and Saturdays, in honor of our Lady. Such fasting was in atonement for one's own sins and those of the world.

Children, after the age of seven, could take part in the black fast. Old people, who didn't work so hard, would concentrate all the more on these practices, not only during the specific times appointed, but throughout the whole year. Since they worked less, they needed less food, so naturally they were the ones to fast more for others. The idea that at

age 59 older people became exempt from fasting never
entered the Russian mind!

Thus, pilgrimages, like fasting, were considered "good
works" before the Lord, ways of rendering glory to God.
Perhaps the most important feature was obeying Christ's
command to take no silver or gold along the way, and to
exist by begging. Everyone dressed alike. One could not
tell the prince or the rich man from the pauper or the farmer.

To the Russian mind, this begging was in imitation of
Christ, who had nowhere to lay his head, and who taught his
disciples to beg for food and hospitality. He also told them
to leave their peace with their hosts and nothing else. To
thus be a beggar, to be humiliated and to practice humility
and simplicity, was another trait of the Russian spirit which
desired so much to be Christlike.

If the pilgrim walked alone, as so many did, the days
were spent in silence, except when he raised his voice in
sacred song. Often, the pilgrims had opportunities to practice both the spiritual and corporal works of mercy. They
might find among their temporary hosts sickness or some
other kind of need. They would often stay to help. It might
be working the farm if the man of the house were sick, or
nursing the sick person, or helping in any other way they
might be of assistance.

They could do this because they were not "on schedule."
When people went on pilgrimages, they never set a time limit,
for they believed very deeply that pilgrimage time was God's
time. Walking as they did, crisscrossing the countryside, they
experienced joys and sorrows, saw good and evil happen.
They thanked God for the good, and when they met evil they
received a clearer vision of why they were making their pilgrimage, and what their atonement was all about.

They meant a great deal to those who were privileged
to offer them hospitality. Such families were brought face
to face with the fundamental truths of their faith. This was

another way that the pilgrims practiced the corporal works of mercy.

I wonder if pilgrimages will ever come to this new world of ours, to this side of the Atlantic. I wonder if young and old will ever "take to the roads" (the little country roads that are left to us these days to walk on), and start walking—slowly, lovingly, prayerfully, silently—for God's sake, for the world's sake, for their sakes. Our new world is also dotted with many shrines.

What a wonderful thing this would be! How much the pilgrims would learn, and how much their guests would learn, for pilgrims must beg for hospitality. Then they would be able to tell us, firsthand I think, about the faces of the North American continent, the faces of its towns, its cities, its villages. Pilgrims usually gravitate toward humble people, toward those who understand what it is to be poor. Yes, it would be exciting if pilgrimages took root in this strange and rootless world, where people whiz by the many holy shrines in air-conditioned cars, equipped with radios and all the modern conveniences of the world. They whiz by the shrines and never even think to bless themselves. Maybe someday there will be books about the pilgrims of North America.

But now, I want to share with you some stories about the pilgrims of Russia. As a child, I remember sitting wide-eyed at the feet of the pilgrims, listening to their tales about God, about our Lady and the Saints. These stories, it seems to me, better than the learned books about the East and the West, bring the soul of the Eastern people closer to the average man. Theologians have their own ways of language and style to discuss the weighty matters of doctrine and dogma. But to the ordinary person, it is the little ways that matter—and the little people. I hope that these tales will help to bring about a better understanding, to all my brothers and sisters of the West, of this mysterious, intangible reality called "the Russian soul."

Russia on the Cross

One pilgrim was an elderly lady. Since it was fall she was dressed in a coarse, hand-woven black skirt and a blouse of wool. Her feet were shod with homemade leather shoes, and on her head she had a black shawl. She also had a Russian parka, lined with sheep's wool inside, and covered with dark, heavy woolen material on the outside. On her breast she wore an icon, the sign of the pilgrim. It wasn't very large. She was in her middle sixties. She had come from a holy shrine of our Lady, and was on her way to her home village some 75 miles from our farm.

The room we were sitting in was lighted with kerosene lamps. A bright fire crackled in the fireplace. Our family and servants were all sitting around the pilgrim, listening to her tale. I was absorbing every word with a heart that hammered against my ribs.

She told us about her travels, and about the wonderful reception she had had at the holy place, the joy that her soul experienced in it, the peace that came to her there. Then she went on to say that on the return journey she had to go through a large forest. And this is what she told us.

"Forests are wonderful places, for many saints in olden days hid there to avoid the persecutions. As you all know, when your soul is at peace and the silence of God reigns in your heart, your whole being changes under his holy touch. Your ears can hear the trees praising God, and the flowers and grass worshiping him. And if you have wept much over

21

your sins and the sins of your brethren, and if you have prayed for the whole world to come to know and love him, then God grants you at times the grace to hear the wild things speak of him to one another. Thus the forests are truly blessed places.

"But as all Christians know, forests are also dangerous places. For the Prince of evil and his angels like the forests also. A Christian would be a fool who did not bless himself thrice before entering a forest. And it is well to hold onto a holy icon when you walk through a forest at twilight or during the night, invoking the names of Jesus and of his holy Mother.

"This I did before entering the forest I am talking about. I was not afraid. The peace of God and his silence were with me, for I had wept in the holy places over my sins and the sins of the whole world. But nevertheless I became uneasy as I went on into the depths of the forest. For I sensed with my whole being that at the moment the Lord was allowing the forces of evil to live in that forest. So, I repeated the names of Jesus and Mary constantly.

"But the ways of God are not the ways of men, as you all know from the book of Job. God permitted him to be tempted. The same happened to me. For before I knew it I heard the trees whisper amongst themselves. Though the night was quiet there was something like a wind going through them. They were whispering in fear and trembling about the Evil One's coming closer. I noticed that the wild creatures of the forest started to run away and hide. I began blessing myself, for the sign of the cross is powerful against the Evil One.

"The road bent a little. Right behind the bend, who stood before me but a man! I didn't like the looks of him. But then, what could he possibly want from a poor pilgrim? Money? I hadn't any, as you well know; we never take any along. Food? I had eaten all my bread and salt, and there was little enough water left in my gourd. So he wouldn't be able to rob me. Nor did he. He was going my way, he said, so he fell in step with me. He did not greet me with the name of Jesus, but he simply called me 'Granny.'

"He asked me where I came from. I told him about the holy place I had visited. He started to laugh and began to talk with a strange wisdom about religion being a superstition fed to us by the priests just to keep us poor and subject to the rich. On and on he went, using big words that I only half understood. But what he said began to sound pretty good; it was true that our people were poor and exploited in many places. Before I knew it—would you believe it?—I was listening to him very intently. Suddenly it seemed to me that what he was saying was true.

"Then he began to talk about Our Blessed Mother. He mocked her. But then, maybe he was not so much mocking her as us who believed that she gave birth to the Lord and remained a virgin. He called it idolatry. Then I knew!

"As you know, every pilgrim carries holy water. We would not travel without it. Quietly, I took out my little bottle. It was getting dark, so he couldn't see what I was doing. I sprinkled him with it in the name of Jesus and in the name of the Holy Trinity.

"Now, you might not believe me, but this is the gospel truth: he screamed. Then he twisted and fell on the ground— then vanished, as if he had never been there at all. But before he vanished he cried out, 'You old fool! All Russia will be covered with rivers of blood over the things I've said. Millions will think like I do. There will be moaning and groaning and tears all over this land. I am out to win it and win it I will. And neither your God nor your Blessed Virgin will be able to save it.'

"So terrible were his words and his voice that I am not ashamed to say that I fell senseless to the ground. When I awoke, everything was dark, and I was scared out of my wits.

I picked myself up, though, and started walking slowly.

"Suddenly there was a very great light on the road, and a young woman, dressed just like me in a pilgrim's garb, with an icon on her breast, came up gently to my side. 'Fear not, Grandma,' she said, 'it is true what the man said, but he was not a man. These things will come to pass so that Holy Russia may hang on the cross with my Son to redeem the world. The only way the world can be redeemed is through suffering with my Son. Fear not. There will come a day when, under the sign of my Son, I will lead Russia to show my Son's face to the world.' Then she vanished too, and I saw the lights of the village."

This story was told to us by the pilgrim woman; I heard it when I was nine years old. You can believe it or not, of course, but this is the way it was told to us on our farm, by the fireplace, those many years ago.

The Woman of Light

A man came to our door one day late in the fall when the leaves had already fallen off the trees and had made a golden carpet on the earth. The chill of the evenings spoke of the coming freezing colds of winter. He was neither tall nor short, neither fat nor lean. He was dressed in the usual plain garb of the pilgrims. On his feet he wore birchbark moccasins so beloved by the Russian pilgrims. His arms and legs were kept warm by linen bandages tied on by intricate patterns of strings. He wore homespun woolen trousers, quilted with fleecy wool inside to keep out the cold winds. His parka also was of the same material, also quilted and tied in the middle with a string on which hung a gourd of water. On his head there was a fur cap, and over his shoulder the pilgrim's bag made of linen, containing some soap and a loaf of rye bread.

He was so familiar a figure that it would have been hard to remember him at all had it not been for his face. It was a thin face, weather-beaten, with eyebrows all shaggy and shot with grey. He had a straight nose, full lips, and eyes that could never be forgotten, not even by a small child like me.

When I looked into his eyes, it seemed that I could look right into his heart. I felt happy, secure, warm and loved. It was truly an incredible feeling to experience while opening the door to a stranger.

As always, I asked him to come in and warm himself by the fire in the kitchen. And, as always, my mother came and served him. Later, when he had eaten, my father offered him rest in one of our spare rooms. He declined this latter offer, saying that he would help with some chores. He worked at these silently, efficiently, all the while his lips moving in prayer.

I myself was counting the hours to that magic time after supper when the whole family would gather around the big kitchen stove. Even the cats and dogs would be there, and we would begin to listen to the pilgrim's stories. Finally, this wondrous hour arrived. His voice was quiet, deep, unhurried. He began to tell us the story of his meeting with our Lady.

His pilgrimage had begun three years ago. He had been a farmer and his wife had died. His oldest son was married. He felt the time had come for him to distribute his worldly goods and begin a life of pilgrimage, fasting, prayer and penance.

This idea of making a pilgrimage—becoming a pilgrim—was and still is (I think) very widespread among Christians of the Eastern Rites. Old age especially is the time for "weeping over the world which does not know Christ." Such tears wash away the stains of sin if they are tears of love, sorrow and compunction. Old age is the time to get ready for death, which to the Russian is but a step into eternal life. Old age is the time to get rid of all the unnecessary possessions and to start on the last lap of the journey to be like Christ. One becomes totally dependent on the hospitality and the charity of others, blending with the poor of the world, becoming to them, as it were, a Simon of Cyrene by one's own poverty, voluntarily embraced.

The pilgrim continued his story. After having divided his goods among his children, he began his pilgrimage across the land, in poverty, recollection and prayer. It was a good life, he said, for it brought him closer to God with every step he took. He felt a wonderful freedom when he freed himself from his earthly possessions and began begging.

He also grew in his love for our Lady as he made his way through forest and dale, visiting the shrines dedicated in her honor. He explained that he kept meditating on the wonders of her being the Mother of God, and how she became the mother of men by standing at the foot of the cross of Jesus. It was very simple to understand this, he said. Since she had given his human body to Christ, and we were members of his Mystical Body, obviously she had to be our mother too.

This mystery, he said, occupied most of his time. There was so much to think about, and our Lady became more beautiful and more wonderful as the days, months and years went by. He loved to stop at her many little shrines that dotted the countryside.

One evening he came to such a shrine and realized that the next village was still far away, and it was late. So he decided to sleep by the shrine, making himself a bed of grass and boughs. After praying before her icon for a long time, he went to sleep.

Several hours later he was suddenly awakened by a child who was inside the shrine, crying bitterly with body-wracking sobs. He got up to investigate and found a little girl of about 10 or 11. Her garments were torn, her one eye was closed, and she had bruises showing on her thin back and shoulders.

He asked her what happened. She explained that she was an orphan, that a family in the village had taken her in after the death of her parents, but that the man of the house drank a lot, beat his wife and her unmercifully, and that tonight he had been on a rampage. She had run away to come and pray to our Lady.

He quieted her tears, shared with her his water and bread by the light of the tallow candle that he carried with him. He prayed with her a little. Then he put her on his green bed, covered her with his cloak and hoped that she would get a little rest. Slowly, still sobbing, she finally fell asleep.

About an hour passed during which he prayed earnestly for the child before our Lady's face. Suddenly he heard a great commotion on the road. A man was coming down, lurching and staggering as he went, shouting and cursing in a loud voice.

In a few moments he came abreast of the shrine and, seeing the pilgrim, demanded to know what he had done with the girl who escaped. The pilgrim greeted him in the name of God, told him where the child was and asked him to leave her alone. He pleaded with him to mend his ways, because he who took an orphan into his house took Christ into it, and to manhandle Christ the way he had manhandled that girl was a grave sin.

The man did not listen. He kept shouting and cursing. He grabbed the child, woke her up, kicked her and told her to go home. The little girl was shaking like a leaf, too frightened even to cry.

The pilgrim, still kneeling before our Lady's icon, was wondering what to do. He cried to our Lady for help. He couldn't fight the man, for he had custody of the girl, and he, the pilgrim, was only a stranger and a passerby. Nor was fighting acceptable in the eyes of God when the weapon of prayer was at hand. Still, he wondered, and he was sad as he saw the man walk down the road, occasionally kicking the little girl and continuing to swear loudly.

Suddenly, a few steps ahead of the man and the child, the pilgrim said he saw a light. Slowly, this light took on a form, the form of a woman—tall, slender and majestic. Her arms were extended, barring the way of the irate peasant.

The pilgrim couldn't tell if the man saw her or not. All he knew was that the man stopped—and then tried to continue on, but couldn't. He seemed nailed to the spot.

Gently, the arms of the woman unfolded and reached down. She took the child into her arms and wrapped her in the red cloak she was wearing. Then slowly, slowly, she rose, up, up, until she finally disappeared in the darkness of the night.

Meanwhile, the pilgrim had fallen on his knees. When he lost sight of the woman he fell prostrate in the dust of the road, shaking as if in a fever. When he got up the man was still standing where he had stopped. The little girl was lying at his feet. As he approached her he saw that she was dead. All the bruises had disappeared. Her blue eyes were wide open. There was no sign of the beating she had received. On her face was a gentle smile. She seemed completely at peace.

The drunken man stood stupefied, looking at the child. He wasn't drunk anymore but now quite sober. As the pilgrim stood watching him, suddenly the man fell on his knees. He covered the face of the child with kisses, begging her pardon. The pilgrim told him what he had seen. The man wept bitter tears.

The pilgrim stayed for the funeral. The man who had beaten her was sent to prison for a time, so the pilgrim later heard. Two years later the pilgrim went to a monastery that had a well-known shrine. Talking to the monks he learned that about a year ago another pilgrim had come and asked for permission to live on the outskirts of the monastery in the woods as a hermit. He said that he had wanted to atone for his sins.

The pilgrim went to see the hermit to obtain his blessing. When he entered the hut made out of tree branches he recognized the hermit—it was the man who had been drunk that night in the episode with the little girl. They didn't say a word to each other. They just bowed low, and gave each other a blessing.

That was the story of the pilgrim with the deep eyes, the one who allowed me to see his very soul. He told it to us one late fall evening, while the wind whistled in the chimney and the glowing wood fire crackled in our kitchen stove.

The Child by the Road

There was Prokoviev. He was a man of indefinite age, maybe 50, maybe 70. He was tall, craggy, with a long gray beard still full of black hair, and with vivid blue eyes, deeply set in a thin-seamed face under bushy eyebrows. The eyes were as clear as the eyes of a child. The mouth was strong. The hands were narrow and always in repose.

He came into our warm kitchen out of a snowstorm. He stood at the door, shaking off the snow from his broad shoulders and stamping it off his felt boots. He took his hat off, and three times he crossed himself, bowing to the icons in the corner. Then, in a low, clear voice, he gave God's greeting to all assembled: "The peace of the Lord be upon this house and upon everyone." Then he begged for hospitality and a bite to eat.

He wore the pilgrim's garb, and had a little icon of our Lady hanging on a string around his neck. He ate, and after supper we all gathered in the kitchen as was the custom and asked him to tell us about the holy shrines and about the stories that were connected with his pilgrimage. He blessed himself, became recollected and silent, then began telling us what he had to tell.

33

He had been visiting the Holy City of Kiev with its many shrines and monasteries. He told of the many graces he had received there and how he had returned and was on his way north to some shrines in the Province of Novgorod.

One afternoon, he told us, the sun had been very hot, the road lonely and dusty. He had decided to rest under the shade of a tree. He fell asleep, and when he woke up it was twilight. But he felt refreshed and decided to go to the next pilgrimage site some 10 miles away. And so he started off.

The road was still dusty, but it was cooler. The road wound its way through meadows and fields. There were no forests, but clusters of trees here and there. It seemed a very peaceful scene. As the night fell there was a bright moon, and he could see very well.

At some point (he did not remember when) he became uneasy. The road twisted and turned sharply, and every time he came to a new turn he felt compelled to make the sign of the cross. Rounding a bend, he saw a man sitting by the roadside. He thought perhaps that the man was sick, so he approached him and asked if he could be of some help. The man said, "Yes. Good." The stranger explained that he needed someone to help him cut his field of wheat. He said he was desperate for help and was on his way to hire someone in the village.

The pilgrim Prokoviev knew that it was not customary to interrupt a pilgrimage except for an act of charity; this might be such a situation. If the man was in dire need, then it would be an act of charity to help him; he would give the money thus earned to the poor. So he agreed, somewhat reluctantly, to help.

The man was most eager. He said, "Come with me and let us begin to cut the wheat right away. The night is very bright and we can see. Tomorrow there might be a storm."

Somewhat astonished, the pilgrim followed the man. The field was not far away. The man gave the pilgrim a sickle and bade him to begin cutting. The pilgrim did so for a spell, but then he noticed that the man was putting the sheaves right away without standing them up to dry. He was putting them on a dray which was hitched to two strong horses. This frightened the pilgrim for some reason he could not put into words. He stopped cutting. Now the wages which had been offered to him were very good.

He asked the man why he was in such a hurry. The man answered sharply that it was none of his business, that he was being paid to just cut the wheat and that was all there was to it.

Uneasy and frightened, the pilgrim began to pray and make the sign of the cross. Immediately, the man, the dray and the horses vanished from sight, and he was there alone holding a sickle.

Trembling, he fell on his knees, throwing the sickle as far away from him as he could. He wondered what had happened to everything! Prayer helped. He arose and went on until he came to the village. He knocked on the first door and was graciously received by the head of the house who fed him and gave him a corner to sleep in.

He had caught glimpses of a woman in the background but had taken no real notice of her. When he was fast asleep he thought he saw someone in the room. He sat up with a jolt and realized that it was the woman, the man's wife. She was very beautiful. She tried to seduce him but he ran away into the night. Shaking like a leaf throughout his whole body, he continued on his pilgrimage, praying unceasingly as he went.

He entered a region of dense forest and spent the next night sleeping under the trees. On the following evening he came across a group of men whose looks he did not like. They journeyed along with him just the same, and they even invited him to partake of their supper when it was time to rest. They made a big bonfire and seemed to have plenty to eat.

When the meal was over one of them began talking to the pilgrim and boasting of all the money they had made by holding up travelers. He opened his coat and showed the pilgrim a pouch filled with silver and gold. He asked the pilgrim to join them for they needed a man of his strength and endurance.

The pilgrim refused. Although he trembled with fear, he bade them good night, and walked away into the dark forest. As he walked he wondered why so many strange things had befallen him during such a short time, and especially during a pilgrimage to holy places.

As he was walking, weeping, praying and wondering, he came upon a little boy who was curled up by the road with a basket of mushrooms and berries next to him. The boy looked tired and weary, and the pilgrim asked him what he was doing there. The boy answered that he had lost his way. The pilgrim took him in his arms and as he lifted him up he wondered why he felt so light.

Suddenly the forest was filled with a great light, and the child said in a clear and gentle voice: "Well done, my servant. I have allowed the Evil One to tempt you three times during the desert of your pilgrimage with the three temptations he uses on all men—bread, women and money. You didn't give in to any of them. Go in peace and tell the story of what happened to all men so that they may know that for those who love me, my grace is sufficient, and that temptations are allowed so that men might grow in wisdom and love."

The light vanished, and so did the child and the basket filled with mushrooms and berries. The night was nearly over. The dawn was approaching. The pilgrim went on, wondering if it had all really happened, or if he had been dreaming. Yet, on he went. Deep down he knew that he had to tell the story in every home that gave him hospitality. And tell it he did.

The Old Man

This is the story of a babushka. In Russian that means a grandmother, an elderly person.

She arrived at suppertime on an overcast November evening. She had on the usual garb of the pilgrim—a black dress, a parka covered in black with a warm, fleecy lambskin inside, the whole tied with a string around the waist. She had *balinkies*—felt boots—on her feet, and a black kerchief tied under her chin. Her face was full of wrinkles, yet somehow they were laughing wrinkles, pleasant wrinkles. She had the bluest, merriest eyes! Her eyebrows were black, though the little you could see of her hair was snow-white. She had all her teeth, and she smiled a dazzling smile.

We fed her, made her comfortable, and after supper everyone gathered to listen to her tales. We were still making pickles at the time, and there were also drying apples hanging all over the big kitchen beams. The air was full of the pickling spices, and the smell of dry apples pervaded everything. The fire in the wood stove crackled as if it were singing a little ditty, very pleased with itself. As usual, I was sitting on the floor at the feet of the pilgrim.

She made a large sign of the cross before she started talking. She told us how she put her house in order before setting out on her pilgrimage. Her son, having recently married, had brought his bride home. She felt that the young people should have some time to themselves, and that this was a good chance to go on pilgrimage. So, having put her corner of the house in order (no one had private rooms in the Russian houses, or only a few had), she took her loaf of bread, her package of salt and her gourd of water, and placed her little savings in the custody of her son. No Russian, as has often been mentioned, took money for a pilgrimage. Off she went, light of heart, with a soul full of joy and a mind full of prayer.

She had left around August. The weather had been good, the people were kind; she had had no real problems. Slowly, reverently, prayerfully, never hurrying, she went from one shrine to another. It was around the end of October that the weather really changed, and it began to rain steadily. The villages were now few and far between.

She was glad to find, one day toward evening, a lonely log cabin at the edge of a forest. The next village was quite far away and she was tired. Humbly, she knocked at the door. It seemed to her that a low voice inside bade her enter. Enter she did.

She looked around for the holy icons that were to be found in those days in every home, even the humblest; they were always in the east corner. Sure enough, they were there. Then, as is the custom of my people, she blessed herself three times, bowed low before the icons in honor of the Most Holy Trinity, and then looked around to greet whoever was there. "Peace be to this house," she said, using the greeting commanded by the Lord.

But the only person she saw was an old man lying in a bed, looking very, very sick. He didn't seem to know she was there. She wondered who it was who had bidden her to enter, but she soon forgot as she busied herself with the fire which was low. The old man looked as if he had been unattended for a long time.

She soon realized that he had a fever. She began nursing him and straightening up the house. There was much to do. The place had been neglected, and so had the old man. There weren't many provisions, but in the barn she found a cow that also needed tending, and a few hungry chickens. It wasn't long before she had the place shipshape, and the man was getting better.

Finally he was up and about. He was still weak, but well, and seemingly very grateful to her though he said very little. He was the silent type! Also, gradually, as she got to know him, she confessed that she began to stand in awe of him. She couldn't explain to herself exactly why, she just did. She especially liked the way he broke the bread at mealtime and handed her a piece, how he poured the tea and always handed her the full mug. There was a certain majesty about the way he did those simple gestures. It reminded her of something—but she couldn't remember what. Eventually she began to think of going on her way. So, one evening, she told the man that she would be leaving in the morning.

The next morning, when she arose, she found the place in perfect order. The kettle was on the stove, boiling for her tea. The porridge was simmering quietly nearby. The table was set—but for only one person! There was no sign of the man. She went out into the barn and to her astonishment found no cow and no chickens. Here again, perfect order reigned, but there were no animals to be seen anywhere.

She couldn't understand any of this, so she returned to the house to look again, but there was only a hall and one room. She had put up a curtain in one of the corners, and there she had slept on the floor, on a straw mattress. There was no one there or anywhere to be seen. She returned to the table to have her breakfast, wondering, and a bit perturbed.

She spied the bible which the man had read from so often. It was open at one page, and, since she could read, she read it. Her eyes fell on the words, "I was sick . . . and you nursed me. Whatsoever you do to the least of my brethren, you do to me."

She began to tremble with great awe. She fell on her

face before the holy icons. She blessed herself many times. Then, since there was nothing else for her to do, she continued on her pilgrimage to the next holy place. But she confessed to us that ever since that experience her feet had wings, or so it seemed to her. She seldom was tired, and her heart sang and sang with great joy, a joy that never left her.

After telling her story, she fell silent. We looked at her face, I did especially. The blue eyes under the dark eyebrows and lashes were as young as a little girl's, even though they were in a face full of laughing wrinkles. A great joy came from that woman. It truly seemed as if her youth had been renewed like the eagle's. Ah, the stories that the pilgrims tell in Russia are so full of wonder!

Russia on Pilgrimage

Some of my readers might be thinking that in these stories I have stressed a little too much the extraordinary, the miraculous elements in the pilgrims' stories. Perhaps I have. What I really was trying to convey is the fact that Russian pilgrims, who still exist and who have existed ever since Russia became Christian, are truly a spiritual phenomenon in my strange, vast and unknown country.

I often pray that the West begin to pay attention, not so much to "how good or bad life is in Russia," nor only to how much steel, uranium, or iron Russia has produced in the last decade; I pray that Westerners are not simply preoccupied with how advanced or behind the Russian school system is compared with the U.S., but begin to take an interest in what Europeans call "the Russian soul."

Strange as this might seem, if the West paid more attention to the soul of Russia, it would understand better all the rest—crops and satellites, education and minerals, production and nonproduction. In my pilgrim stories, I tried to present some facets of this many-sided reality called "the Russian soul."

The Russian pilgrim is a symbol for the whole nation. Russia herself today is on pilgrimage. She is heading toward the goal which has been in her soul for a long, long time, ever since she was baptized in the name of the Father, the Son, and the Holy Spirit.

The Russian people hold in their souls a vision of a

society that lives in love and peace and which lives by a
strange equality based on that love. A community of equals
where everyone is truly a neighbor to the other in the fullest
sense of that word.

To anyone who is familiar with Russian history and
Russian religious thought as expressed by its writers, artists
and its simple, grass-roots people, it will become evident that
the Russian people have again and again tried to achieve the
implementation of this vision.

It took a wrong turn someplace. There was much confusion and bewilderment in Russian history which justified
that wrong turn. But there is another crossroads ahead. At
that one, or perhaps the one after, Russia will take the right
turn. It would be well for the West to understand this.

For the Russian spirituality is a spirituality of concern
for the neighbor. This is exemplified by the way in which
they celebrate the Eucharist, or, as they say, the Holy Liturgy.
Their form of celebration bespeaks their deep understanding
of the Mystical Body of Christ, and of their communion with
the whole Church Suffering and Church Triumphant.

All throughout Russia's history, the people, in their
spiritual life and worship, have felt deeply their responsibility
for their neighbor. The second commandment has entered
the very marrow of their bones. Few Western writers or politi-
cians have paid much attention to this. Yet, Communism, in
its pristine purity, offers a shadow, albeit a dim shadow, of
this concept.

Russia is on pilgrimage, seeking the shrines of love, the
shrines of God with a hunger that is deeply and, I believe,
permanently buried in its mysterious soul. Russia today is
also a suffering pilgrim, even a crucified one. Strange as this
might sound, a crucified person can pilgrimage very far. Even
in the awesome silence of pain, a fruitful dialogue can take
place. Painful whisperings and moanings can preach the
greatest sermon.

But I am afraid that the tremendous lessons of this crucifixion and this silence are escaping the West, just as the lesson of that other Crucifixion escaped those who witnessed it. For me, there lies one of the greatest tragedies of the modern age. Russia is being analyzed by the West in the laboratory of its intellect, with cold objectivity, even as human beings are sometimes now analyzed in our modern hospitals. But no doctor, scientist, or pathologist can capture the essence of a human being. Unless attention is given to the soul, the very core and heart of a person is not seen. All our scientific equipment will not give the complete data.

So it is with the West. It has Russia under the microscope of its intellect, and so it continues to baffle. The data is incomplete because the essence is being overlooked: the soul of Russia on holy pilgrimage.

II

Stories of Today

The Blue Door

As I look back over the years gone by, I see much that needs writing about, if only to show that there is nothing mysterious about the lay apostolate or its life. For it is, on the whole, a very ordinary life. Its only glamor is that it is lived entirely *for God's sake*.

Yet its very ordinariness is perhaps the most extraordinary thing about it! Its life is spent in the marketplace of the world. Nothing, either in clothing or manner of life, distinguishes lay apostles from the people among whom they try to witness to Christ by sharing their lives, their joys and sorrows, their pains and gladness. They blend with everyone so that their true weapons of poverty, chastity and obedience may all the better lead others to the immense *caritas* of Christ whose heralds they are. *To love God and to prove it to him by truly loving one's neighbor and spending one's life in serving him*: this is the very heart of a dedicated lay apostolate; this is the "witnessing to Christ" that changes the world.

How is this witnessing to Christ, this loving of God and man accomplished? This I will try to tell to the many who have often asked me to do so. And it seems to me that the best way would be to tell you some stories which will bring the works of the apostolate closer, make them more alive and real than perhaps a learned treatise would do.

For the lay apostolate, in a manner of speaking, is a replica of the house of the Holy Family in Nazareth to which all neighbors, I feel sure, were welcome. Their home also stood in the very heart of the marketplace of that holy village, blending with all around it so as to become part and parcel of its rhythm of life.

48

So I place these humble little stories at the feet of Mary, the patroness of all lay apostles. They are her stories as well as mine. Sometimes an idea comes to nestle in a human mind and will not be dislodged until it is given birth in writing, painting, music, or some other human creative expression. This is exactly what happened to me as I thought over the many wondrous stories of God's grace and mercy and of our Lady's tender love that occurred in our lives, and continues to occur.

There are many ways of thanking the Lord for his many gifts to us. It seemed to me that my way should be by recording in story form the true happenings—the adventures in grace, as Raissa Maritain called them—of God's mercy.

A visiting priest once asked why all the doors of our foundations are always painted blue (which they are). I answered, smilingly, "because of a very old, old saying of my people: 'Every front door painted blue in honor of our Lady brings her blessings on all who pass through it.' "

So, here are my "Blue Door Stories." Many people have passed through our blue doors, each receiving, I know, Mary's blessing and her Divine Son's grace and mercy. The blessings were not always visible, but when they were, they were beautiful to behold, joyful to witness, encouraging us and helping us to persevere.

I would like to share this "joy of beholding" with all those who love Christ the Lord and his Mother; with those too who do not yet love them because they do not know them. These are the stories of the many blue doors which all blend into one—the blue door of our Lady through which the extraordinary ordinariness of our daily life can be seen.

A Drama of Faith

It was just one of those days, no doubt about it. Cold, blustery, with the thermometer falling with a frightening rapidity. It was especially frightening to us, members of the first Canadian Friendship House, which, like most of our houses, was a flimsily built structure, open to all the vagaries of climate. It had a big Quebec heater right in the middle of our library and main workroom.

That Quebec heater ate coal like a starved man eats bread. It shed an intense heat at a circumference of about three to five feet, leaving the drafty corners colder than ever. There was also a big range which demanded even more coal. It was used to cook meals three times a day, but threw off little heat. The guests were many during that severe weather of early depression time. They came in the hundreds, which did not help the heating problem much!

Yes, it was one of those days, and the heater was eating voraciously. The cook had just informed us that he had enough coal for his range for about two more meals. He doubted very much there would be enough for the stove and heater both. He presented the last scuttle of coal which he had painstakingly gathered from the coal bin, and that would be that—and what did I propose to do about it!

Some 70 pairs of ears listened to this question with a particular personal interest. They were among the guests whom we called Brothers Christopher. Most other people call them bums and panhandlers. They had made it a habit to

51

spend the extreme cold days of the winter in our Friendship House, reading, chatting, smoking, or just sitting around quietly and enjoying the warmth and coziness of the place. Our house was always open to them, and they were sure to meet there some long-lost buddy they had left in Calgary, Halifax, or Edmonton, waiting his turn to take his next chance with the freight cars and the railway detectives.

Yes, the news spread fast that there was no more coal; it was a matter of vital importance to all of us. No coal, no heat; no heat, no food. And what was I going to do about it! (Our bank balance was not enough even to buy one more scuttle of coal, let alone a ton or half-ton which the emergency called for.)

Prayer was the only answer I knew of, a prayer of trust in God and in his divine providence. So, slowly, but clearly, I told the cook and the assembled brethren that we would have to ask God for the coal, ask him simply, humbly, in utter faith, adding a little postscript that "because of this emergency and the falling temperature, we need the coal *today, before four o'clock in the afternoon.*" The scuttle of coal would not last any longer.

Just as I started to get on my knees to pray, and as the cook (a non-Catholic but already trained in our prayer ways) started to get on his knees, a shuffling of chairs announced that all the Brothers Christopher, whatever their faith, were ready to join us.

Suddenly, a deep, mocking voice made itself heard, challenging my statement about praying to God. He advised everyone to drop this foolishness, which is what prayer was according to him. Anyone in his right mind knew that religion was the opium of the people and nothing more. I realized that once more we had a Communist brother in our midst.

Paying no attention to his continuing tirade I knelt down and in a loud voice prayed an Our Father, a Hail Mary, and a Glory Be; then I stated our needs to the Holy Spirit, the Father of the poor. I added a short reminder to Mary, his Spouse, about the deadline of four o'clock! I then sat down at my desk and went on with my letters. The cook went back to the kitchen. And the knights of the road, who all had joined me in prayer, returned to their cards and conversations.

Our Communist friend would not let it go at that. All right, he said loudly, everyone had prayed to a Deity that did not exist. So he would stay until four o'clock to witness our utter defeat and to enjoy our discomfiture when that blasted coal did not arrive. He would also check on me, and see to it that I did not phone some benefactor for the fuel.

And he went on. It was high time to cure people of all this foolishness. *I* was beyond redemption, of course, but he hated to see these good men (all members of the down-trodden proletariat) be so hoodwinked by my silly faith in something that never was and never would be.

I listened quietly to all he had to say, and then asked him what he would feel like and what he would do *if the coal arrived on schedule!* (This was quite apt to happen in Friendship House where a hundred emergencies, including the three daily meals, were miraculously taken care of every day.)

He thought my question over for a while and then said that, if this happened, he would look into the matter of religion and God, with as open a mind as he could muster. The situation being what it was, this was equivalent to a public promise.

For the space of a minute or two a dead silence reigned. The ticking of our old wall clock could be heard like the voice of doom. Then, everyone once again went back to what he was doing—everyone except me. I made a pretense at writing. But all I could hear above the hum of conversation was the ticking of the clock. Had I been too presumptuous? Had I overstepped the bounds in showing my inner certainty that God and our Lady would hear our simple prayer and answer it before four o'clock? Could one do that, set a time limit on God's providence?

Round and round these thoughts danced their fandango in my head. With all my heart I wished that I could go to the church around the corner and talk to God about this unexpected predicament. But that would not do. No. Our Communist friend would suspect that I went to beg or buy the coal. No. I had to sit tight, sit it through. I had to look "unworried."

Slowly at first, then faster and faster, I started to make acts of faith. I pleaded with Mary for the coal, now not only because of our need for warmth and for food, but also because a man's soul was involved. And all through my silent prayer the old wall clock marched on, ticking away its amens.

Dinner brought a welcome diversion. Even washing the dishes helped. Then, it was 2 p.m. I went back to my desk— silent, somewhat afraid, yet still believing.

Three o'clock. Three-twenty. The last vestiges of coal dust went into the Quebec heater. The range had long been cold. From the kitchen a nasty draft was beginning to be felt. The cook came into the library, carefully closing the kitchen door. His supper was all prepared, but there was no heat to cook it.

Three thirty-seven. A quarter to four. Ten minutes to. The Communist laughed and started to harangue the silent, morose crowd of men. My heart felt heavy, and my soul darkened for a moment. Of course, I had been presumptuous.

Five minutes to four. Three. The voice of the "orator" became a pain in my ears and tears were close to flowing.

One minute to four—and the front door opened with a bang! A dirty-faced man with a dirtier paper in his hand stamped off the snow and vigorously inquired if this was Friendship House. He had, he said, orders to deliver a ton of coal! Would someone look sharp and help him put it where it should go. After all, he didn't have all day to deliver it!

The old clock struck four. Never had its hoarse, wizened old voice made such music in my ears. No other sound was heard. No one moved. The coal driver stood still and looked around, bewildered at the quality of the silence that greeted his impassioned request. I'm sure we must have seemed deaf and dumb to him.

Suddenly, as at a bugle call, everyone was moving, shouting, coming and going out to help get that ton of coal into the coal bin we had built in the back yard.

When the coal was in and we were alone, the now silent Communist and I sat and looked at each other. Slowly he got up, looked at the crucifix before which we always kept a vigil light burning, and said, distinctly and clearly: "Nazarene, you win again."

Not long ago I received an invitation to an ordination. I could not go because it was too far away. Anyhow, it would have cost too much to travel there. But I was there in spirit. The occasion was the ordination of the man who did not believe that God could send coal to his tired and freezing children in the Toronto slums. Alleluia!

Peter Maurin

The telephone rang insistently. It had been ringing all day for we were expecting Peter Maurin of the Catholic Worker to come for a lecture. He was also expected to speak at St. Michael's College. But as yet there was no sign of him. The Catholic Worker, when we phoned long-distance from Toronto to New York, had told us that he had left for Canada more than a week ago!

Of course, with Peter Maurin, anything could happen—and usually did. He was that kind of apostle. An article that someone wrote about him once was entitled "On the Bum," and that described him very well.

He would start for a city in the north and perhaps wander all through the southern part of the continent to get there. So I was not too worried. But the college was, and so were many people who were anxious and eager to hear this extraordinary man speak. Hence the busy phone.

This time the call had definite news about Peter. He could not phone himself, the caller said. He was being "detained" on the Canadian border by the immigration authorities. It was one of the officials who was calling. He wanted to know all about Peter. His official voice droned on and on, asking all kinds of questions. We were wondering where all the money would come from to pay for his collect call!

We answered as patiently as we could under the circumstances. Suddenly, the voice changed tone, and became the voice of a normal human being instead of an official. "Lady," he said, "off the record, is that guy a madman or a saint? I am a Catholic myself, but there he sits in the Immigration H.Q., surrounded by all on duty, telling them about God and the Catholic Church—things I never heard before. It sure is interesting but, you know something, if what he is saying is true, I have a lot of reading up to do. How about it, lady?"

I assured the rather worried voice that Peter was okay, on the way to sanctity and not madness—unless the madness was the madness and folly of the cross. Then I asked if Immigration would let him in. Yes, they would, if we came and fetched him and would take responsibility for him while he was in Canada. We said we would. It was then somewhere around 11 p.m.

More phoning—lots more. We got a driver and a car and off we went to Windsor, arriving in the wee hours of the morning to find Peter. We found him, happily discoursing about God while he ate a substantial meal of coffee, sandwiches and doughnuts provided by the Immigration boys. They were all standing around, with somewhat dazed expressions on their faces, listening to him.

Formalities over, we hustled Peter into the car and brought him back in time for Mass and breakfast. It was good to see him come through the Blue Door. It gave him its benediction, and he brought us his. Peter Maurin, "the poor man of the North American Continent," cofounder of the Catholic Worker movement, inspiration of thousands, was, to my mind, a veritable saint!

I had met him before. But on this occasion he was at his best. He spoke in blank verse of God and Mary, of Jews and Gentiles, of justice and injustice. In sharp, concise and precise phrases, as only his wisdom and knowledge could mold them, he spoke of heaven and hell, of workers and management, on the whole social scene and the apostolate of the Church. He spoke of what he really knew. He was that perfect combination of student and worker.

As I listened to him, I thought how much we of Friendship House owed to him and to Dorothy Day, and to their family of the Catholic Worker. I doubt if I would have persevered in the apostolate were it not for the help of these two burning apostles of God and of his love.

Peter had brought me the vision of the whole that day. To all of us, in fact, he made it crystal clear that we were all *responsible for the state of the whole world* everywhere, for each person individually and for all collectively. We all in fact *were* our brothers' keepers.

Under his clear exposition, the doctrine of the Mystical Body became luminous. Peter was like that. He could take sublime verities and, unwrapping them from the heavy garment of words with which centuries had clothed them, he brought them forth into the light of day.

Peter is dead now, his body rests in a cemetery near New York City. But he lives in the hearts of the thousands who knew him. He lives on in the souls of the thousands who never saw him but who feasted and who keep on feasting on his *Easy Essays*. (These are still available for a dollar at the Catholic Worker, 223 Chrystie Street, New York, N.Y.)

To me personally he is vividly present. I remember him often when I pray. Simply, as I used to do, I ask his advice on many things concerning the apostolate. Yes, it was a blessed day when he passed through the Blue Door. Friendship House became richer for his passing. Peter Maurin, pray for us!

The Pity of God

The priest who walked through the Blue Door one day was very young. He had really blond hair which kept flopping over his eyes. There was a boyish quality about him that somehow enhanced his earnestness and priestliness, and cast a strange radiance into the room which, as usual, was filled with Brothers Christopher, lolling at ease in the fairly hard chairs.

Many got up when he came in, but he motioned them to remain seated and made straight for my desk. After a very brief greeting he laid his problem before me.

It concerned a family in his adjacent parish. The father was a Communist and the mother a practicing Catholic. There were seven children of school age. The father would not allow them to attend the parochial school, and he forbade his wife, under pain of bodily injury, to even set a foot inside a church. All were reluctant to have recourse to the law because of their love for him.

The man was a Slav. His English was halting, but he spoke Russian. Would I go and see if, with the help of the Holy Spirit, I could do something with him? He, the priest, would then follow up on the situation.

I arose and followed the priest, first through some of the shabby streets of our slum area, then into an alleyway, until we came to a dirty little shack, but with a beautifully kept garden.

The priest pointed out a man chopping wood by a little

shed as the person I was to talk to. Then he left me, with a whispered blessing!

I approached the busy man and greeted him in Russian. He smiled as he answered. We began to talk. But slowly, as the real content of my message began to penetrate his mind, the smile changed into a scowl. Then anger became a kind of macabre dance in his eyes. Suddenly, he became furious.

Raising his axe, he shouted that he would brain me right there and then if I mentioned God or Church once more. Gathering up all the tatters of courage that remained, I went on slowly to try and show what he was doing to his wife and children.

He lifted his axe and started for me. I ran. I ran as I had never run in my life. Past garages and garbage cans that got in my way. Down alleys that seemed, for a moment or two, dead-end traps. Suddenly I stopped. Why was I running from a man who thought he hated God? God loved him! He *had* to be made to see that!

I turned around and saw him, panting and disheveled, still holding his axe high. He was turning into the little back alley where I was. He stopped in front of me. We stood there, looking at each other intensely.

Fear had left me. An immense pity took possession of me, and I wept unashamedly. Slowly, like a child caught in an act of mischief, he walked closer and closer, shuffling and dragging his feet. Then he stopped, and asked why I was crying. Was it from fear? I told him no. It was from sorrow and pity for what he was doing to Christ.

Suddenly he fell face down into the dust and dirt of the alley. He sobbed deep-heaved sobs, the tears of a strong man. Strangely enough, I found myself praying to St. Paul, for this figure prostrate in the alley reminded me of Paul of Tarsus. Neither of us spoke, neither made any gesture. Time seemed to stand still.

The man arose and, dropping his axe, stretched out his

hand and shook mine. I went home through the labyrinthine ways of the slums. He went back to his home surrounded by flowers.

Several weeks later the eager, boyish priest came to find out how I had persuaded the Communist to send his children to the parochial school and allow them to go back to church—how in the name of all that is holy had I gotten him to the point of even going to church himself!

I did not tell him the whole story. I simply said that it was the pity of God, which for a fleeting instant had taken possession of my heart. It was the pity of God that had brought him to make those decisions. I still believe that this is so.

An Ordinary Man

There was nothing to distinguish him from the thousands of others who came through the Blue Door every day to ask for clothing, food, shelter, or some other sort of help. There was about him only that strange air that goes with being poor. He was quiet, about 28 or 30. His clothes were shabby, mended neatly. His shoes were scuffed. His hair was a little too long, but then, a haircut costs money.

When he spoke, the voice and words were those of a well-educated man. A sense of tragedy deepened around us as he spoke. As he continued speaking, the scene became even bleaker.

He was a Protestant minister, he said. He had had troubles with his faith and had left the church where he was pastor. Now he was just drifting, unmoored, searching for . . . what? He couldn't exactly say. He was all alone in the world. No kith or kin. The Depression had made it difficult for him to get a job. He was a greenhorn at manual labor; besides, the job market was glutted now anyhow.

He hadn't eaten for quite a while, and he was a bit "tired." He had seen the sign over our door—Friendship House—and had come in on the spur of the moment. He needed friendship perhaps even more than food and rest.

I noticed the deep lines of tiredness and mental weariness that his search had etched in his young face. I realized that the man was starved, sick and truly exhausted. Food and a clean bed were ready in a jiffy.

Two weeks passed before he could really say he was back on his feet. He stayed with us and worked willingly and efficiently at any job we gave him from scrubbing the floors to peeling potatoes to serving the Brothers Christopher. He was always quiet, self-contained, listening more than speaking.

He became a confidant of many a Brother. He was that kind of man. Then, one quiet winter evening, when the Quebec heater was roaring cozily and the wheezy old clock was counting time with little spurts and coughs, he came to my desk and sat underneath the crucifix. The rest of the room was deserted. The vigil light threw little shadows on his clean-cut face.

In a low voice he stated simply that he had found out what he had been searching for. Catholicism was the answer. It held the fullness of truth and he wanted to embrace it. Could I arrange for instructions?

The vigil light suddenly flared up. A coil in the heater fell with a clank in the stillness of the room. The sound broke the profound spell of gratitude that was welling up in my heart. I took his hand and held it for a minute or so. I said nothing. What was there to say in the face of such a miracle of God's grace?

We found a priest. There was a big cake baked with loving care by Mr. Pritchard our chef, complete with candles. Joy and laughter echoed in the big library to celebrate. Paul stayed on, and did his work even better than before.

The occasion arrived for another cake—this time with flowers as well as candles. And there was even more joy and happiness in our humble home. The wanderer, the seeker, the "bum," the Brother Christopher was leaving us to study for the priesthood. He was going to the seminary of an austere order.

Recently I visited him. He has a beard now. There is in his face a peace that truly surpasses all understanding. His eyes somehow reflect a joy that seems uncontainable. The former minister, the Knight of the road, the Brother Christopher had come home, via the Blue Door. Paul was one of seven who entered the priesthood through this Blue Door. Through the infinite grace of God, out of the thousands of Brothers Christopher who came to us, seven became other Christs.

But then, why should I be so amazed? Anyone who passes through a door painted blue in honor of our Lady gets her special blessing. With that, anything can happen! And marvels did happen, and miracles become as commonplace as what most people call "coincidences." "Daily I remember Friendship House in my Mass," the bearded priest said. No wonder Friendship House is blessed.

A Woman, a Child and Christmas

His shoulders were thin and hunched over, like those of a man who never in his life had had a warm coat to shield him against the biting winds. It was as if he had always tried to make himself narrow so there would be less for the wind to whip around.

His face was long, thin and sort of transparent. His eyes were blank and terrible to behold. He was like a blind man who was seeing. Emptiness, with endless, frightened depths, could be found in those eyes if you looked long enough, but few bothered.

He made his way to the Quebec heater in the middle of our big room. Taking off his hat, he twisted it absentmindedly in his hands which were extended toward the pleasant heat of the strong fire. The men looked up from their game of cards, or from their newspapers and magazines. All sort of nodded or smiled. He did not seem to notice. He just stood there, twisting his hat as before, hunching his thin shoulders, and warming himself.

I got up and made my way to the man. I asked if he was hungry. He nodded yes, as if he was too tired to speak. I led him to the back room, our kitchen, and placed some food before him. He sat down. He ate wolfishly, as one who needed food desperately.

Then suddenly he wept with deep, racking sobs that foretold the rushing waters of a dam about to break. I sat still. The pain of Christ encompassed me as it had for years.

Thousands like him who had come through the Blue Door had brought His pain to me, to us, that we might take it away from them, and take it into ourselves. That is what loving the neighbor really means—becoming the bearer of his cross of pain, sorrow and need.

Then, just as suddenly as he had begun to cry, he began to speak. The story he told was simple, sordid and old, yet somehow it was poignant, new, full of pain. For when a story is connected with a human being, with real life, it is never old, sordid, or simple.

He had married much too young. She became pregnant. He became frightened of the poverty all around them. He abandoned her. That was six months ago. Then he could not live with himself. He went back because she was alone, young and defenseless. All around about was the big Depression. No jobs. Besides, he had returned too late. She had vanished and left no traces, at least none that he could follow.

He did not care after that. He became a sort of bum, riding the rails—but always in search of her, his abandoned wife and child. The baby should by now be several weeks old.

Where was she? Where were they this Christmas Eve, the feast of babies and of mothers? He lay slumped, his head in pieces of bread and peanut butter, the upset bowl of soup trickling its contents onto his thin overcoat and onto his tightly clenched hands. A naked heart is difficult to look at. I left him for a while. Later I saw him warming himself by the stove. His eyes were dry again.

Slowly the place emptied out. It was Christmas Eve. One by one the tired and weary, the young and old, the poor and destitute—and those who had become poor for love of them—all were going to midnight Mass in a nearby church. The young man with the empty eyes did not move. So I decided to stay and share his loneliness and his emptiness. There was always the morning Mass to go to.

A strange, hushed silence settled upon us. I put out most of the lights and put on the lights of the big Christmas tree that stood by our large window. The place looked a little bit like a chapel, with its vigil and Christmas lights. Then, I lit the lonely candle in the other window as a welcome to wayfarers, another custom of my faraway country.

Still the young man did not move. Slowly I began my rosary. What else could I do before the silent drama of a man's soul on this holy night but pray? The snow was falling fast and heavy. Hurrying passersby were but shadows outside the warm circle of our room.

Without warning, the door opened. A woman with a baby wrapped in a shawl stood framed like a picture, the snowflakes on her melting quickly in the heat. I stood up to greet her, but the young man was quicker. He had turned and saw her. He almost jumped the space that separated them. She was quickly in his arms. He was repeating the woman's name over and over again. The baby began to cry. Then everything was silent.

The Virgin with the vigil light flickering on her face seemed to come alive. The silence was profound. Then the bells of the church nearby rang out their glad news of the birth of the Child. The thin man with the hunched shoulders had found her whom his heart was seeking.

I gently closed the Blue Door she had left open in her excitement and went into the kitchen to finish my rosary.

The Prostitute

The girl was a prostitute, she never denied it. In fact, she seemed to flaunt it. She would loudly demand to be served ahead of the long and patient line of people waiting for clothing because, she said, she was tired of "standing too long after her night's work"!

Of course, she didn't get that attention, for justice to others had to be guarded and priorities observed. So she would curse, in a steady, droning monotone for over an hour or more, until her turn finally came to examine the clothes we had and to select the things she needed. Somehow the obscene words sounded strange coming from her, for she was young and beautiful. Admittedly, it sounded as though she had had a lot of practice!

Often the line of patiently waiting people would shuffle uneasily under the impact of her profane deluge of words. Often, too, passersby would hurl insults back at her. But she simply went on cursing, oblivious to the waiting line, the city, oblivious to everything but her desire to get to the head of that line.

At long last her turn would come and she would step through the door of our clothing center, a storefront which opened onto a busy slum street. The worker in charge was a young and beautiful girl. She had to listen to this stream of filth for over an hour every day of the week—except Sunday! She bore it patiently.

Funny, how serene that worker's face was, how gentle

and understanding she always appeared. Every day she would suggest a cup of coffee to the girl to help take the coarseness out of her throat. Always the girl drank the coffee and then, very critically, looked over the secondhand clothing we had to give away until she found what she wanted.

Three hundred and sixty-five days in a year, minus Sundays and holidays. That gave our worker about 300 days to listen to abuse, make coffee and give out a dress to this girl. That's a lot of hours, a lot of days, a lot of abuse, a lot of coffee and a lot of love!

Then one day the prostitute was sober, quiet, watchful and even a little timid. She knocked politely and entered when bade. Then, standing straight and tall, she looked into the staff worker's beautiful face and asked point blank why she had been so patient. Why hadn't she called the cops? Why had she so sweetly endured insults and injuries? Why had she given her the coffee, the dresses, the polite and gentle service? Why had she never complained?

Having spent herself with questions, she stood quite rigid, as if bracing herself for an answer she was afraid to hear.

All the worker said was, "Oh, that's very simple. *I love you.*" The prostitute swayed as if struck in the face, and out of her very soul came the cry, *"Me! Why?"*

Even gentler than before came the reply: "Because you are Christ to me, because he died for love of both of us, because I am your sister in him, because I am here to love and serve you."

The girl crumpled to the floor. She wept with deep, heavy sobs that slowly subsided, leaving her spent and quiet. Slowly she got up. She said: "I never heard such things, but I know you mean business because . . . because you were always the same. There was always the coffee, the dresses . . . yes, now I know. I want to love as you do. Teach me how."

The girl was a prostitute. She never hid it. She flaunted

it. But after that day she took instructions. She was eventually baptized and went to confession and received Communion. Today, in that big city, there are 17 of them that I know of, prostitutes who wept at the feet of Christ. They all arose, cleansed and whole, and it was this girl who had brought them to him.

"There Is No God"

It was the height of the great Depression. As usual, gathered in our big library, were the men whom the world considers the dregs of humanity—bums and hobos. To us of Friendship House they were Brothers Christopher, travelers on the road of life, closer to Christ perhaps, in their utter poverty, than many others. They were sitting around our table. The lamp, placed in the center, made strange shadows on their faces, now revealing, now hiding the souls within.

The staff worker in charge was sitting behind a desk that overlooked the whole room, writing letters. Some men were reading, others were just sitting or resting, allowing the warmth of the room to soak into their tired and weary bones. A few played cards in a corner. Two were engaged in a whispered conversation. It was just an ordinary evening in Friendship House during the Depression.

Suddenly, the door opened, and a tall man with a weather-beaten face and a mane of white hair entered. He wanted to know if he was late for supper. The worker reassured him that, though he was late, there was enough left over to warm up for him. So both disappeared into the back of the building where we had our kitchen and dining room.

In the meantime, in the library, the hum of conversation grew louder. When the staff worker and the white-haired man returned, they saw a priest sitting at the head of the table talking to the men. The conversation seemed to be rambling, but in reality it wasn't.

73

It was the custom in Friendship House at the time to invite daily some priest from the city to visit with the men and to talk about God and the things of God—or about whatever the men felt like talking about. The topics were plentiful. The men looked forward to this hour of discussion, so friendly and simple. Few of them, alas, had had any close contact with priests. Most of them on this occasion seemed interested in what the priest was saying.

After a while, the priest would rise and with an encouraging smile inform everyone that he would be upstairs in a little room if anyone wanted to go to confession. There were evenings when nobody went, other times when one or two walked wearily up the creaking stairs; sometimes a great many went. The joy of it was that there was a priest waiting, right there at Friendship House, where the men felt somewhat at home. At our place few people harassed them, and the police left them alone, for a while anyhow. They could relax.

This particular evening the discussion went on longer than usual; it was because of the man with the white beard. He stood in the middle of the room, warming his back against an old-fashioned coal stove. He towered above everyone else because of his height and leanness. In a well-modulated voice he attacked everything the priest had to say. He bewildered many and egged on others to join in his arguments. Voices grew louder and tempers began to fray.

All at once the man with the silver white beard drew himself very erect. His shadow made a strange background for him. In a clear voice, carefully enunciating every word, he said, "Father, all this is nonsense. There is no God, and I will prove it to you. I'll challenge him that if he exists to strike me dead here and now."

For a second there was a profound silence. The weight of it was crushing. But it only lasted a moment or two. Then, the man with the silver hair gasped, moaned and began to clutch his throat as if unable to breathe. Then he fell, face downward, crashing like a huge tree falling in a clearing from the axe of a woodsman.

For the space of an "Ave" no one moved. Then all bedlam broke loose. Some of the men brought water. Others tried to loosen his clothes. The priest bent low, trying to hear a heartbeat. Someone called a doctor. *But the man was dead!* "Dead," said the doctor, "from heart failure."

While ambulance drivers, doctors, police, neighbors and curiosity seekers shuffled in and out, the stairs leading to the little room upstairs were creaking, creaking under the weight of some 50 men who were going to make their peace with God—the God whom the man with the white hair had so openly denied and challenged. From evil God draws good, and from death, life.

A Son of Israel

He was tall, thin and double-jointed. I discovered the latter when, having come through the Blue Door, he chose for his seat the small, narrow typewriter table that stood—typewriterless—next to my desk. He placed himself on it, Moslem-fashion, and looked most comfortable and relaxed.

We talked easily. I liked him. He was young, and had the long, gentle face of a poet, a dreamer, a student. We ask few questions in Friendship House. We have found out that this is the better way. There is something sacred about a human being that must not be violated by mere curiosity. It is to be reverenced and loved.

In the course of our slow, random, yet friendly conversation, he told me he was a poet, wrote for the *New Yorker,* and was a Jew. An Orthodox Jew. I was glad with the strange gladness that always comes upon me when a son or daughter of Israel passes through the Blue Door. I never forget that we Catholics are, spiritually, all Semites. Christ was a Jew, so was Mary, his Mother. The Church was born from the open heart of a Jewish man who was also God. I love Jews.

He stayed for supper but ate little. He could eat only kosher food and we had none. He continued to talk, slowly, beautifully, about many things. He was filled with charity, and he warmed with his love our little Madonna flat in Harlem. He was worth listening to. We all prayed together the official evening prayer of the Church, Compline. Some-

76

how he made the psalms of David come alive for us. He recited them with so much fervor.

We were sorry when he had to go, but then he came back again, and again as a volunteer of Friendship House. He helped with the Brothers Christopher, with our youth paper, and with our little class in journalism. He did everything very graciously, but not always efficiently. He could be rather absentminded at times! It didn't matter. *Caritas,* otherwise known as Love, spoke loudly in his every gesture. It shone in his face and spoke through his words. We began to love him more and more.

One day he startled me: he asked if he could become a staff worker and live our strange way of life. It was a way of utter poverty and complete dedication to what was known then as the Lay Apostolate of Catholic Action. At first I did not answer, but begged a little time in order to pray over it.

That night I wondered how this could come about. Ours was a fully *Catholic* way of life, and he was a Jew. And yet . . . and yet . . . how could I refuse such a shining soul, one that would bless everything it touched?

There was only one thing to do. That was to see the Ordinary of the diocese and ask his advice. That's what I did. I shall never forget the warm, paternal smile of a great man, nor his words: "Catherine, how can we refuse the son of our Mother? You know that we are all, spiritually, the children of Abraham. Take him with my blessing and see what happens."

I did. It worked out well. The young man took his day off (Sabbath) from Friday evening until Sunday morning. Then he worked Sundays while we rested. He was very punctilious in dealing with Catholics, always giving them the right kind of literature, always directing them to someone who could help them with answers if he couldn't. But most of the time he could because he was well-educated, and knew the Catholic faith in an intellectual, abstract sort of way.

There was, of course, the difficulty of learning many things, like mopping floors! The first time he was given the humble task he departed with mop and pail across the street to the storefront he was suppose to clean. An hour passed. Then two. He was still there.

Sheer curiosity overcame me. What could a man be doing to a floor that ordinarily only took 30 minutes to get clean? I crossed the street, opened the door, and stood transfixed. All the water in the pail was on the floor. He was standing in the water, the dry mop upside down in his hands. He was using it to write on a piece of brown paper. He was scribbling (I learned afterwards) a beautiful poem about mops, floors and clean soapy water!

Gently I asked him what was going on. Startled, he whirled around, and, with a slight blush, acknowledged that since he didn't know how to mop a floor, he thought a poem about the work would make up for this deficiency. I told him it certainly did not. (We printed the poem afterwards, and I taught him how to mop a floor!) There were many incidents with this son of Israel, but I'm afraid it would take a whole book. He is the kind of man about whom someday books may be written.

One day, almost a year and a half later, he left us. His health began to fail, mostly because of our poor fare. He did not write us too often. Once in a while I would get a letter with funny little illustrations, usually a short letter. It would make me strangely glad. Once in a while I would answer in the same manner.

Years later we had a celebration at our Chicago house. It was the anniversary of its foundation. Bishop Sheil was the guest of honor. He gave a little speech to a large audience of our friends. In explaining what Friendship House was, the bishop related a story from a recent visit to a Trappist monastery.

That Abbot had asked the bishop what Friendship House

was. "A tall, thin, Jewish man," the Abbot said, "had come to him and asked to be baptized. It was due, he said, mostly to a place he had come in contact with called Friendship House."

The Bishop went on to say that for those who knew Friendship House, the Jewish man's story needed no more explanation. This Jewish man was Bob Lax, the friend of Thomas Merton, who describes him so well in *The Seven Storey Mountain*.

Yes, I love Jews greatly because Christ was a Jew and so was Mary, his Mother. In Bob Lax I saw both the child of Abraham and the Son of Mary—both Judaism and Christianity. Alleluia!

Aunt Dilly

Her hair was snow white, but her deep blue eyes were young, young with an eternal, merry youth. She was well-dressed. Looked like a schoolteacher or a nurse. She walked through the Blue Door quietly yet firmly, as if she had a definite purpose in mind. She asked for me in a clear, musical voice untouched by the years which had left lines on her face.

Sitting across from me at my desk she stated her purpose tersely and simply. She was a retired schoolteacher. She lived on her pension. She had saved a modest sum which she had originally planned to give to an order to have Masses said for the repose of her soul. For she was an orphan, with no kith or kin. She wanted to be sure that someone prayed for her after her death.

But she had heard me lecture and decided to give us the money to use for our work in interracial justice. It was not too much, but it was all the extra money she had. She had a strong feeling that Christ in the Negro, whom she saw clearly and desperately wanted to help, would look after her soul. It was only after this that I noticed the utter simplicity of her attire and the quiet shabbiness of her garments.

Her elderly face was serious, intense. Her young eyes smiled joyfully, flooding the room with mute alleluias of gladness. I accepted the offer gratefully, knowing that I was privileged to be seeing a great miracle of grace. For the love of God that gives of itself and all it possesses so generously is a grace beyond reckoning.

Quietly she made out the check. She handed it to me and was about to take her farewell when I suggested that she stay and have supper with us. That was the beginning of a long association between "Aunt Dilly" and us. She became a volunteer in Friendship House, Harlem, and all the people of those changing and restless days knew her well.

Children followed her lovingly, begging for stories which she told with infinite skill. She had the power of keeping the young ones sitting still and absorbed for hours. No small power! Young people came to her with their heartaches and growing pains. They nicknamed her the "Aunt Dorothy Dix of Friendship House."

Adults also of all years came to her with their joys and sorrows. All she had to do was walk through the Blue Door and the word would spread up and down the teeming streets that Aunt Dilly was at Friendship House. All sorts of people flocked to her.

Quietly and unobtrusively she brought many back to the sacraments; she straightened out many a marriage. She never seemed to get tired and was always willing to help.

She had a little side job. She was a graphologist. She read handwriting for banks and department stores in their personnel sections. She analyzed our handwriting, too, describing accurately to each of us our general characteristics, our weaknesses and our strengths. She rarely made a mistake.

Once, spying a letter of mine on the desk, and also one from Eddie Doherty who had just discovered Friendship House himself, she calmly remarked that, "objectively speaking," the man who wrote that note and I would make an ideal married couple. Our handwriting, she said, revealed a complementarity. A year later I was married to Eddie Doherty. Aunt Dilly was right again!

One day we learned that she was ill. No visitors were being permitted. Then she died. Half of Harlem and all of Friendship House were at her funeral. Many priests whom she had gotten to know from contacts with us were also there. All of them remembered her shining soul in their Masses.

Aunt Dilly lives on in the hearts of many. She lives on in our hearts and in our prayers. If Christ will repay us for giving even one cup of water, what will he not do for Aunt Dilly who loved so many so much.

Shepherd Out of the Mist

He was of medium height, with a head of thick, iron grey hair that made him look very distinguished. There was about him also an air of authority, a clerical air, that made me stand up quite spontaneously when he first came through the Blue Door and entered our warm library. He shook off the snow that covered his well-tailored coat.

For a moment he puzzled me. That moment quickly vanished when he introduced himself as the rector of a Unitarian church in a big Western town. He said that his reason for coming was the desire of his congregation to have me lecture on the subject of "Christianity and Racial Justice."

While we are discussing dates, fees and all the details pertaining to such a transaction, the sadness of his eyes attracted me. There was in them a pain I could not define. Somehow it called out to me in a soundless voice that brought a kind of despair into our peaceful library.

We settled the details of the lecture. He assured me that I was free to speak in my own "Catholic" fashion. In fact, he said that his congregation was particularly interested in the *Catholic* approach to this vital question. The lecture would also be an open one. That is, it would be held in a hired hall with admission open to the general public. We invited him to stay for supper but he refused, saying that he had a train to catch. As I escorted him to the door, the feeling of sadness once more took hold of me; once more I had to shake it off.

In due course, my lecture tour brought me to his city and to his congregation. Mindful of his wishes, I tried to present, in utter simplicity, the full Catholic viewpoint of the matter. The lecture was well received. Many questions were asked. Great interest was also shown in regards to other aspects of our faith. Finally, the meeting came to an end and the Rev. Minister and his wife took me to their home, the hospitality of which they had so graciously extended to me beforehand.

After a light lunch, his wife retired. He asked me if I would mind coming into his study for a little chat. There was, he said, something on his mind that he wanted to ask me about. Gladly I accepted.

The study was lined with books. The table indicated a man who read and studied much. Notes covered the whole top. Books with odd bookmarks overflowed onto the chairs and even onto the floor. The furniture was utilitarian but comfortable. I sat in a big leather armchair beneath a shaded lamp. He sat facing me, seated on a hard swivel chair near the desk.

I waited expectantly for his questions. Silence greeted and enveloped me. It was a strange, disturbing silence that somehow I could not break. I continued to wait for him to speak, but he remained silent, motionless, as if lost in thoughts that were carrying him far, far away.

The silence became more intense. Then it became extremely heavy, mingled with darkness and fear, but pregnant with expectation. I began to pray to Mary for the grace and strength to endure this strange and painful silence.

Suddenly, it was broken by him with a sob and a cry wrung out of the depth of his heart. Like a wounded man he fell to his knees. He whispered that, perhaps in a minute or two, I would run out of the room and out of his house in sheer loathing and horror. He was an ex-priest! Yes, an ex-priest!

Time stood still, and the silence descended again. But now it was a different silence. It was the silence of utter pity, of compassion and of love. Slowly I arose and gave him my hand. I called him "Father" and made him sit down again in his hard swivel chair. Then I talked quietly of Peter and Paul, of God's mercy, and of the fact that there was no such thing as an ex-priest. A priest is a priest forever, no matter what he has done. I added that, though he did not know it, he had passed through our Blue Door, and that anyone who did so received a blessing from our Lady.

The next day I left. Years passed. We of Friendship House prayed daily for a "special intention" though I alone knew that the intention was for this lost shepherd.

One day, a thin, white-headed man came through the Blue Door. His face seemed familiar. He was dressed in the clerical black of the Catholic clergy. There was in his eyes such a serenity and peace that I stood still for a whole minute or two, my hand extended in greeting. Then he smiled, a slow, slightly sad smile, and I knew who he was.

It was the shepherd. He had come especially to obtain the blessing of Mary and her Blue Door before leaving for one of her monasteries. He said he was joining the monastery of Our Lady of La Trapp. He hoped to spend the rest of his days as a Trappist. He blessed us and, for the last time, went through the Blue Door: a shepherd who had come out of the mist.

I leaned against the door and watched him go down the street. Then I turned and impulsively kissed the wood of that blessed door. The children playing on the street looked at me rather strangely.

Four Dirty Pennies

When I think of all the people who have come through the Blue Door, my heart is filled with gratitude. This is especially true when I think of God's little ones, the *anawim* who often are known only to him.

I remember only the first name of the person whose story I am now going to relate. Maybe she never had a surname! Yet, I remember *her* very well. Every Saturday, rain or shine, cold or hot, she would come through the Blue Door. She would enter oh so softly and close the door gently behind her.

Slowly, with tired step, she would walk up to my desk, and, after a few words of greeting, lay on top of it in a tidy row four dirty pennies. Then she would explain, almost in a whisper, that this was all she had left of her pay to give to Christ in the poor. Then, with a little smile and a bow, she would ask for our prayers. Slowly, bidding everyone present a soft good-bye, she would walk out through the Blue Door, closing it very gently as she had closed it coming in.

She was a Negro, a widow. She earned her living by scrubbing a few office floors at night. Her name was Martha.

She brought her four pennies every week for four years. Then, one Saturday, she did not come. I never saw her again. Months later someone along the street told me about a poor woman who was buried in an unmarked grave in a potter's field. I asked the woman's name. All they could remember was that her first name was Martha. Her surname? Nobody seemed to know.

God Knows

She told me haltingly, and a little shyly, that she wanted to help me help the Negro. What could she do? I looked at her and loved her with a great love; I have loved her ever since. She never realized the gifts that she brought me that day. But God knew, for without doubt she was his messenger.

For on the murky afternoon she came, I was alone in my dark apartment which that day somehow seemed darker than usual. The loneliness of Christ ebbed and flowed all around me. It encompassed me so utterly that I literally cried out. I could not take another minute of it. I thought I would pack and leave this hell on earth where man's inhumanity to man could be seen in every face I encountered along the treeless, crowded, dirty and segregated streets.

Then, suddenly, there she was. Miss Russell. Softspoken, shy, yet, shining from her lovely light brown face was a charity whose other name is love. My thirst drank its fill from this inexhaustible cup. There was a deep repose in her quiet ways, and I felt refreshed. There was peace in her gentle speech which was punctuated by a warm, friendly silence. I was healed of my pain and my fears.

I led her across the way into the rectory basement where we had our first "clothing center," and to which many "naked" came to be clothed. It was depression time in Harlem. The door of the clothing center was painted blue.

Fifteen years later Miss Russell was still there. She had walked quietly into our hearts one murky afternoon and asked to help the Negro. After 15 years she was still there, still walking softly. Few people noticed her working, fewer still will ever know about her. But God knows. Through her being there, I was blessed, and all of us in Friendship House were blessed. Just a simple, quiet person who wanted to help. Not famous. God knows.

Katzia

She was a little thing, with a plain face and red, awkward hands too big for her size. She washed dishes in some third-rate restaurant for many hours of the night. Her accent was thick and her English was bad. She came to see us because she had lost her job and was hungry. It was the lovely blue color of our door that had attracted her. She could not read English very well, she confessed, but she could read the welcome color.

She stayed with us for a week or two. Self-effacing to the point of anonymity, she went about cleaning whatever needed cleaning, scrubbing whatever needed scrubbing, without ever being asked or told. Then, one day, she found a job and moved away.

Monday was her day off, and she spent it with us. Often we knew it was Monday just by seeing her walk in, dressed in light, cheap clothes. They never seemed warm enough in the winter nor cool enough in the summer. She would immediately get busy by helping with the most menial chores. She was usually silent, except for a word or two or a fleeting smile. She always left at closing time and we never knew her address. Her name was Katzia, Polish for Catherine we thought.

One day at Friendship House she met another girl, a thin, tired child of about 19 or 20 who had been a prostitute. The looks of this girl had utterly deteriorated under the impact of her "tiredness," and she had just drifted into Friendship House. So many people just drifted in at that time. They had no place else to go. Women were sleeping on the floor, and often there was no more floor space.

Katzia took the girl by the hand and off they went into the fog of a November afternoon. We heard later that they were living together in Katzia's room, wherever that was.

Katzia didn't come to us on her day off for several weeks. We tried to locate her but couldn't. A few months later we received a letter from the director of a sanatorium. It was a dictated letter, signed by Katzia. She said that she was a patient there along with the girl she had tried to help.

As one person we all went to visit our Friendship House auxiliary. We were just in time. She had contracted TB from the other girl through their sleeping together. Both were very, very ill. A year later Katzia died and the thin girl got better. She has been working ever since, without pay, in the convent of some poor nuns. "Greater love has no man . . . ."

*   *   *

These were three stories about three of God's *anawim,* his little people. Many more such came through the Blue Door, and their stories are known only to God.

The Man with the Deep-Seeing Eyes

One day a young man with a very interesting face came through the Blue Door. He was neither very tall nor short. Medium. He had a charming smile and eyes that took in everything they saw. They seemed to see very deeply. I remember his eyes.

He didn't come alone. He came with Bob Lax who had earlier come through the Blue Door. Bob introduced him as a fellow poet, writer and teacher.

We sat for a while and talked. It developed that he had been on the campus of St. Bonaventure University in Olean, New York, and had heard me lecture there.

Teatime arrived in our storefront in Harlem. I had introduced this idea. Because I was a Russian I could drink tea all day long. The Negroes didn't like tea too much. If we had coffee the four o'clock tea break became an American coffee break!

I asked our new friend if he wanted to do some work while at Friendship House (it was our custom to offer visitors something to do!). I forget what he "volunteered" to do— filing library cards or something like that. But soon he had to leave and he made his departure.

I didn't expect to see him again, but he came back often and talked about many things. He talked about interracial justice and poverty, of God and the things of God, of religious vocations, then back again to poverty, personal poverty, Franciscan poverty. Every time he came he invited me out, as he said, "to be able to talk without interruption." It was true, the interruptions were constant in our storefront. So he took me out to various eating places, not only to "feed my face," as the saying goes (we had so little exciting food in Harlem), but especially to talk.

In between these "outings" he came more often to Friendship House to offer his services. His teaching job in the winter in Olean precluded too much work at our place and the "spiritual outings," as he called them, were reserved for Saturdays or Sundays.

One day I said, "Look, my friend, this is fine and dandy, but I just can't keep going out like this and eating steaks when our staff are eating the eternal soup. And our neighbors, they aren't exactly rich either. I also think we have had enough spiritual conversations to clarify whatever it is that you want me to clarify. Why don't you try out this poverty, this way of life you are always talking about? Instead of teaching, come and join Friendship House in Harlem for a spell, or maybe forever. How about that? I guarantee you will know much more about spiritual dimensions by living with us in Harlem than by talking about it over steak, good wine and cheese for dessert. As far as I'm concerned, I'll be praying for you—but no more discussions away from Harlem."

I didn't see him for quite a while. Then suddenly he appeared and announced that he had decided to join us. He didn't know for how long, but he had left his job and here he was.

Poets, writers and teachers are great people, but all of them seem to have, at least in the beginning, a complete inability to concentrate on practical things. My new friend wasn't very much different from Bob Lax, but I will say that he learned faster. Lax was more of a dreamer. It wasn't long before his friend could mop a floor with the best of them, and even scrub it at times when necessary. He washed windows, looked after the clubs, led interesting discussions with the Brothers Christopher who passed by or with any other person who needed to talk or have someone listen.

Yes, it seemed he fit in very well. At this writing I can't remember if he stayed with us three months or more. I do remember that a priest came to give us a day of recollection. He spoke beautifully on the lay apostolate, on the need for the laity to participate in the life of the Church more actively and more deeply.

The day after, my new friend came and said, "Catherine, I have made up my mind. I am going to enter the Trappists in Louisville, Kentucky. As I listened to the retreat master yesterday, everything suddenly became very clear to me."

I was very happy that he finally had found his real vocation. I knew intuitively that those eyes which took in everything and which saw deeply, that those eyes could look into the eyes of God even in a storefront in Harlem.

Before he left he put into my hands a manuscript and said, "If you can peddle it and sell it, the royalties are yours." I tried to "peddle it" among some Catholic publishers but no one would accept it. So, I put it away in a filing cabinet somewhere. Eventually it was brought to Madonna House in Combermere with all our other records and files.

The manuscript proved to be a rough outline of what later became *The Seven Storey Mountain*. Many years later, I came across the manuscript that the now-famous Thomas Merton had given me those many years ago in Harlem. I wrote him and asked him what he wanted me to do with it. He gave me the name of his agent. She was so happy it was still in existence. She had been looking for it. It was later published under the name of *The Secular Journal of Thomas Merton*. If you read the foreword of that book, you will learn more about the relationship between me and this young poet, writer and teacher who came through the Blue Door one day only to leave it and enter another door that belonged totally to our Lady!

A Christmas Story

It was a sort of upside-down affair that came floating through my memory when I began to write this story. The memory was of a Christmas night. It seemed upside down because no one came through the Blue Door that night in Harlem.

I had just closed it behind the last of our bunch. We had had much to finish up before Midnight Mass. That's when I met the strange trio that I most assuredly did meet that night. They did not go through the Blue Door but, some-how—and don't ask me how—the Blue Door was certainly involved.

It was a perfectly natural meeting too, nothing mirac-ulous about it or about anything that followed. And it was a nice meeting, one that made Christmas Mass a little more joyous and the meditations that followed a little more pro-found.

Just as I was leaving, and had turned from locking the Blue Door (which had given me some trouble that night I confess—the key stuck or something) I was confronted by a very handsome Negro man of middle age and a small, younger woman. Evidently she was his wife, and she was holding a baby in her arms. I could not see the baby's face. It was all bundled up against the raw, New York wind that was blowing into a gale.

Very politely, the man lifted his hat and, in the soft accents of the deep South, he told me that he and his wife

97

were lost in this big city. They had just gotten off the train. He was a carpenter, hoping to get a better job than the one he had had in the little village they came from. But, with one thing and another, they had been delayed en route. They didn't have any money, that is, not quite enough for a night's lodging. Perhaps I could tell them where to go, what to do, and to whom they might apply for help.

Having said his piece, he stood relaxed, politely and silently waiting for my answer. His wife, who had never said a word, just smiled once or twice at me. She stood as confident and as still as he, sure that I was just the person to help them.

Before my mind's eye came a vision of the telephone. I almost turned back and opened the Blue Door to try and contact some social agency that would attend to their wants. Then I looked at my wristwatch. It was almost 11 o'clock, and on Christmas Eve! Whom could I find at this time? And where? And if I did, this poor family would have to brave strange subways. I could, of course, send them by taxi. I did have a few extra dollars in my purse—wonder of wonders. But the Family Shelters of New York separate families sometimes, because of lack of room.

Lack of room! Christmas Eve! Man, woman, child! It all suddenly hit me right between the eyes. Of course, I knew it was *just a coincidence.* Nice, in a way. But so many people came to Friendship House just for this kind of help and information. No, this was not the time to send such a family anywhere. This was the time to offer them personal hospitality, if for no other reason than to atone for the hospitality that was not given almost 2,000 years ago.

Of course! Why hadn't I thought of it before! There was what the staff workers of Friendship House called the "Hermitage," that is, my room. It was so many things in one. It had a desk, a bed, a gas stove complete with oven, and a refrigerator of sorts given by the management; it even worked sometimes. The room also contained a sink and laundry—a full-grown laundry tub. Yet, all in all, it was a cozy place, especially that night. I had been given a tinseled Christmas tree about six inches high. It was a far cry indeed from my lofty, native Russian firs, so stately in their majestic beauty.

The little tree, nevertheless, was nice, very nice. I had placed under it a miniature crib. When I came back from Mass, I had intended to place the Infant there. Yes, the room was spic and span, and very, very, cozy. Why not invite the couple to spend the night there? Tomorrow I could contact the needed agencies.

No sooner thought than done. My strange couple was still silent, courteously waiting for an answer that surely must have seemed to them a long time in coming. But they showed no signs of impatience.

Slowly, and for some inexplicable reason rather diffidently, I invited them into the hermitage, apologizing for its humbleness and its being many things in one. Their smiles broadened. The woman straightened herself and somehow looked taller as she pressed the child closer to her. The man voiced his thanks and proceeded to follow me.

Thus we walked the three rather long blocks that separated the Blue Door from my quarters. No one said a word. Yet, the silence was companionable.

Once in the room I made them as comfortable as I could. The baby, finally out of its wrappings, was lovely. I had not heard it cry. The man said it was a boy, their firstborn. I made them coffee, fried some eggs, set the table, and then told them I would peek in after Mass.

It was one of the most beautiful Masses I ever participated in. The thought of my three pilgrims snug in the cozy room probably made it so. Personal hospitality to strangers, to Christ, warms him who gives it so much that it is a blessing in itself.

The Mass over, I rushed back to my room. To my

astonishment I found the front door ajar! That is never done in Harlem where one uses several locks just in case. (It is the same wherever there are tension, segregation and poverty.) I pushed the door open. The room was empty.

The dishes had been washed and stacked away, each where it belonged. No signs of occupancy were left whatsoever. The Infant I had meant to put into its tiny crib under my tinseled tree was already there, and a candle was lit in my window!

Gun and Gun Moll

The phone on my desk rang sharply. I don't know why, but all the phones of Friendship Houses have a note of urgency in their rings. Of course, this might just be my imagination. Anyhow, this time it most assuredly did!

As soon as I picked up the receiver I recognized the familiar voice of a priest who always had urgent reasons for calling. He asked this time if I had room for two people. One was a man just out of prison. He had been serving a sentence for manslaughter. It would have been murder if the victim, a bank teller, had died from wounds inflicted on him during a holdup by this man. The other person was his girl friend. Both had been sent to the priest. They had no money. He did not know exactly what to do with them—until he thought of Friendship House.

None of us had ever met a murderer before, not even one who failed to kill his victim. Nor had we met what the more lurid magazines call a "gun moll." But there is always a first time in Friendship House for meeting all kinds of people. Since we had room, and they were destitute, and they belonged to Christ, of course, I said, we would be glad to have both of them.

In a few hours the Blue Door opened and in walked a man with a tired, haunted face, and a young girl, all paint and paste. She had a cupid's bow vividly outlined on her lips, mascara on her lashes, dark red eyebrows, nails dripping red—and fear hidden in deep, blue eyes that could not have

101

looked on the world for more than 18 years.

I welcomed them warmly and went back to the business at hand. We were counting pennies, nickels, dimes and the occasional quarter that had come from selling our little paper, *The Social Forum,* at the doors of many churches.

The man surveyed the piles of cash with a practiced eye and declared that I was foolish to keep so much cash in the house, especially as the neighborhood was not the kind where cash should be displayed so lavishly. The girl was chewing gum and kept making strange—but not unmusical—noises.

I agreed with the idea of caution, but went on to explain that there wasn't much money there; secondly, that everyone around here knew where it came from; thirdly, that many of the hoboes—Brothers Christopher to us—had helped to sell the paper; and fourthly, that many of our neighbors took a lively interest in the proceedings and their results.

The man shook his head unbelievingly and announced that, in return for food and shelter, he would guard the money with his life! With that grand statement he produced a gun and moved his mattress close to the desk drawer in which we had rather "carelessly" put the "take."

It was time to get settled for the night. Those of the Brothers Christopher who were then living with us went upstairs. The gunman made himself comfy. We took the girl to the house next door where we slept. I wondered what we would find the next day. We found the room neatly swept, the mattress tidily put away, the gun out of sight—and the money in the drawer intact.

The girl, refreshed by a long night's sleep, washed clean of paint, and dressed in a simple gingham frock we had found in our clothing center, looked very young and demure.

They stayed a week. Both made themselves useful around the place. She loved to sew, and he liked to cook. No one spoke to them about religion, about the past, or even about the future. Those of us who live behind the Blue Door had learned long ago that love often expresses itself best in an infinite and tender silence, especially when dealing with those deeply wounded by life or by the indifference of their brethren in Christ.

Within a week the man got word from what he rather generally referred to as "home." We bade them Godspeed and put them into Mary's hands as we do all those who pass through the Blue Door.

Years passed. Then, one day, a large limousine stopped in front of the Blue Door of a Friendship House in another city. A man whose hair was very white stepped out. There was a great kindness in his eyes and a big smile on his face. A woman walked behind him, quite evidently his wife. Her face was beautiful in the full maturity of middle age, un-marred now by any paint or makeup.

She held a boy of about six or seven by the hand. Last of all was a girl of about 10 or 12, with one of the most beautiful faces we have ever seen.

The man approached our desk. Silently, he placed on it a check for a thousand dollars. Then he smiled and said, "I have wanted to do this for a long, long time. It is a little token of my gratitude for all the hospitality, love and trust that I found in your place many years ago. But this is only the first payment to Lady Mary who has blessed us ever since we passed through her Blue Door."

Yes, he was the gunman who had watched over our money with his trusty gun. And this woman was the gum-chewing moll! How wonderful—and how wonder-full were the mysteries of grace which passed in and out of our Blue Doors!

Dom Virgil Michel

On a blustery, dark March day in the early thirties a priest, now dead, walked into Friendship House through the Blue Door. He was young, but he was carrying a flame within him. I know this is a strange way to talk about anyone, but that was the impression he created. Zeal, understanding, eagerness to be about his Father's business, and a love of souls that shone through every word he spoke—all these added up to one word: flame. Perhaps I mean fire, the fire that renews the face of the earth.

Most assuredly we needed a fire on that March day of long ago. That day marked the end of the first half year or so of our first foundation. Our souls were filled with darkness and with a storm of doubts and temptations against this strange new vocation to which we were trying to give birth.

True, we were feeding the hungry, clothing the naked and so on, but these needs of our brothers in Christ were overwhelming us! The weight of ridicule, spoken and unspoken, in high places was literally crushing us. No one, it seemed, except our saintly bishop, even dimly understood what it was we were trying to *be* before the Lord and to *do* for him.

The day was indeed dark when this fiery priest, a bearer of light, warmth and truth walked through the Blue Door. He proved to be a person in love with the flame and fire of the Holy Spirit.

His name was Dom Virgil Michel. He was a Benedictine monk from the now-celebrated Abbey of Collegeville, Minnesota. It was later to become the heart of the liturgical movement in the North American continent, the beats of which were just then beginning to be heard.

How does one begin to voice gratitude? How does one begin to thank another human being for opening eyes that were still partially sealed? That day Dom Virgil Michel gave us postulants and novices in the then-unknown novitiate of the lay apostolate the *vision of the whole*. He showed us the *whole Christ* who was not crippled by compromise or touched by the fear of human respect. He showed us the Christ who demanded of those who wished to follow him utter dedication, a burning love, perfect obedience, acceptance of his cross and a joyous, unflinching stability.

Yes, how does one go about thanking a priest of God for all these things? Yet, he did not stop there. Lavishly he fed us with the Bread of Truth and the Wine of Love that were his own food. He went on, illuminating the darkness of our weary minds and leading us into unsuspected depths, into that vision of the whole that is born from the vision of the whole Christ.

This vision, he said, begins with the Mass. Only there could we find the whole Christ. Slowly, majestically, before our eyes (it seemed as if he were mixing the spittle of his words with the clay of his burning charity and unsealing our blindness with it) he unrolled the whole lay apostolate as being first and foremost our own *being before the Lord*.

Empty chalices that we were, we first had to be filled by Christ at Mass. The Mass. Sacrifice and Sacrament. Food and Drink. Sea of Fire in which to plunge and become oneself a fire. Bridal Chamber, where the Bride, the soul of men, enters to become one with the Bridegroom, Christ.

And the fecundity of the Mass. *Ite, Missa est.* Go, live the Mass and you will restore the social order and the world to Christ—but first begin with yourself! That is the soul of the apostolate. That is your soul. That is your vocation. Be steadfast in it, persevere and Christ will use you to renew the face of the earth. You will become pregnant with him, give him birth, allow him to grow to his full stature by the process of his growth in you and your corresponding death to self. You will be his hands, his feet, his eyes, his voice, his heart! He will walk the earth again in you, for this is the hour of the laity.

Yes, a young Benedictine priest said all this in the early thirties of our hopeless century. He said it in a shabby storefront of a big-city slum to a small, insignificant group of lay people who were crushed by the darkness of misunderstanding, ridicule and inner doubts, and who did not know which turn to take on that fearsome first crossroads of their destiny.

Years later, in 1951, kneeling at the feet of the Father of Christendom, I heard the same words repeated. The Pope's last sentence seemed to echo and reecho in the vast room where our interview took place. For a split second they seemed to blend with the vibrant voice of the Benedictine now dead: "This is the hour of the laity. Persevere. Be steadfast and you shall renew the face of the earth. God needs you. The Church needs you. We need you."

"Dom Virgil Michel, we of Friendship House cannot truly thank you enough. The whole Christ, him whom you possess now in the fullness of reality, he thanks you for us. All we can say to you must be said in pieces, slowly, day by day, hour by hour, minute by minute, second by second. It will be said by our lives, our thanks incarnated in them. For without your fire *there might not have been a Friendship House at all!*

"Father Virgil Michel, I who am the only one of us left who heard your living voice that day, I give you my life in the apostolate of Friendship House as a token of my inexpressible gratitude. And I pray that you may place so small a gift, so tiny a token of my love for him, into his Sacred

Heart. Big or small, it is a love that grew out of the *vision of the whole* that you gave us on that blustery, dark March day so many years ago.

"One more thing, Father Virgil. Ask the blinding Flame of Love in which you now dwell to send more tongues of fire, like you, onto this cold earth. Priests burning with zeal for souls. Priests who are flames of his divine love. Priests who have but one desire—to be other Christs! We need them in the marketplace, Father Virgil, desperately!"

John of Our Blessed Lady

Every city has them, those strange men with long hair and unkempt beards that haunt various churches. They kneel, usually in the front pews, seemingly lost to their surroundings, praying, dreaming, or just kneeling. Living statues.

Who are they? No one seems to know. Few people care to find out. Most laugh at them. Are these men psychos? Few people sit close enough to them to be able to find out. They smell of the great unwashed. And, who knows, if you get too close you may carry away with you some live memento of these strangers! These lonely men live as mere shadows of the big city. One of them came through our Blue Door one day.

It was a late spring day, the time when the light seems to linger and is loath to let the night take over. It is the time when twilight slips in while night and day are discussing their rights. Time is standing still, being neither night nor day. Things are shadowy, less real somehow. It was the time when it was both too early and too expensive for us to put on any lights. It was at such a time that John walked in.

He had on dilapidated slippers with toes sticking out here and there. He wore an indescribable garment that in better days might have passed for a frock coat. Tied around the waist with a string, it covered his thin frame. The frayed cuffs of trousers could be seen peeking out from under it. His long hair fell in cascades of rich brown and blended with a beard of the same color. His hands were clean, with long, tapering, aristocratic fingers which clutched a huge 15-decade rosary.

Out of the twilight he came, like some man from a far and distant land. He bowed low before the big crucifix that hung on our wall. Then he bowed to the assembled company—the staff of Friendship House and the Brothers Christopher. Then, quietly, he knelt in a corner and began to pray his rosary.

His voice was soft, low and cultured. Every word came out distinctly, beautifully, well enunciated. He did not ask anyone to join him, but for some reason we all did. It was a long rosary but it didn't seem long. When it was over we offered the visitor some food. Smiling, he declined. But he promised to be back. Then, bowing to God and to us, he went out and vanished in the darkening twilight that was now almost night.

Spring turned into summer, and summer gave way to autumn and to cold, sleety rains driven by chilling winds. John returned every week. And every week, like a ritual, he went through the same gestures and his 15 decades of the rosary. Those present always joined in.

Lady Poverty lived with us then. Coal was rationed just so, enough to heat the place but never enough to make it really warm. The building was old. Through the cracks in the walls where my desk stood the wind whistled its icy tunes. Half the time I felt chilled to the very marrow of my bones. One by one our staff and many of the Brothers succumbed to more or less severe colds. All recovered. Then I got sick. It took me by surprise. One minute I was well, the next minute I was shaking so much that my teeth rattled. I was cold. Then I started burning with a fever.

An hour or so later, in bed, I alternated between fever and chills. I remember very little of what happened, except that, according to those who nursed me, I kept praying for coal and complained that there was too much of it! I screamed from a pain I do not remember having felt. Perhaps I could not feel anything because my temperature was above 105°, or so they said.

I had two big abscesses in my ears. A doctor finally ordered me to the hospital. The staff was frantically phoning our many friends, trying to raise funds for an ambulance. That is how I had to go, the doctor said. It was the 10th day of my illness.

All arrangements had been made. The hospital bed was ready. The ambulance would be here at 7 p.m. It was around 4 p.m. of that day that John walked in. To the astonishment of all he asked how I was! He had not been at Friendship House during all those 10 days of my illness. Many voices told him the news all at once. I was to be operated on at the hospital in a few hours.

For the first time since spring John spoke at length. He calmly announced that all this was unnecessary. All that anyone had to do was to join him in the rosary and ask our Lady to cure me.

Sheepishly, the staff workers and the Brothers Christopher—some 75 people were there—looked at one another. John knelt down and started the beads. All joined in. This time he said them very slowly. Almost an hour passed, I later learned, before they were through.

The time was 5 p.m. In the meantime (again, I later learned) I was tossing, screaming, moaning and acting like a soul possessed. I was delirious, I suppose, and oblivious to everything. At 5 o'clock sharp, so they say, I screamed once more louder than before. Then I turned around and fell asleep.

At 6 o'clock I woke up, demanded food and wanted to know what all that pus was doing on my pillow. They took my temperature and it was normal!

The doctor was sent for. After an examination he announced that the abscesses in each ear had burst, evidently simultaneously. I didn't need any ambulance. I didn't need any hospital. I didn't need any doctor. In a few days I was up and around and entirely well.

No one saw John again. I looked high and low for him to thank him for his prayers. But once the Blue Door had closed behind him he never came back.

Of course, every city has them, strange men with long hair and matted beards. Men who pray for hours in empty churches. Who are they? Are they psychos or saints? Few people seem to know or care.

I have never forgotten John of the cultured voice who once came through the Blue Door fairly regularly to pray his long, long rosary. A modern Joseph Labre? Perhaps. I called him John of Our Blessed Lady.

An Ordinary Miracle

This is a story from our Canadian countryside, at Madonna House, Combermere.

The day had been hard. The bed was so wonderful. Sleep was instantaneous and deep—deep but far away. Faintly, faintly, it seemed that someone was calling me. That someone was shaking me! No, they couldn't do this to me! I was too sound asleep! It would be a sin to wake me!

But it was no dream. They were actually waking me. I opened my eyes and saw my husband and the doctor. They were saying that I must get up to help a certain woman. She lived far away. Her time had come for her baby and it would be a difficult one. The doctor was worried.

Half asleep, half awake, I got up and somehow managed to dress. I was still in a dreamy state as I got together the things that I needed and started out into the night. The air felt cold. I was glad to get into the doctor's car and try to sleep. The car sang a lullaby of tires against the asphalt road. Suddenly, the song of the tires changed into the sound of sand crushed by the weight of the car. We must be off the road, bogged down.

I got out and looked around. We were mired in a rutty country lane. The heavens were full of stars, the frogs were singing, and spring was everywhere in the air—spring and new life. But the ground was soft and full of icy water. The whole road was one muddy lake.

The doctor got out too and after a time was convinced

that the car could go no further. He picked up his case of instruments, I picked up my nurse's equipment, and we started walking. We had, I judged, a mile or so to go. The doctor walked ahead and I followed.

We saw a light bobbing up and down like a will-o'-the-wisp. It turned out to be a kindly neighbor come to give us his oil lantern. I tried to light the way but there was no way to light! We were walking over fields, up and down hills, now on solid ground, now ankle-deep in mire. The beauty of the night was a song around us, but the walking grew harder and harder. From a ridge the lights of a town shone like a thousand glowworms. But that town was far away.

Finally, at the bottom of the last hill, a tiny house nestled. Leaning sideways, it peered at us with one sleepy, drab eye—the dim lamp in the window. A quarter of a mile down the slope and we were there.

The kitchen was big. A man and a woman waited for us and a wee baby in a homemade crib. The woman's time was nearly here, but not quite. We must wait. So we waited—the man, the woman, the doctor and I, and the little mite in the crib.

What a strange waiting that was! Tiredness filled my bones and slowly crept up toward the heavy eyes and the nodding head. Yet, sleep would not come, because there was a woman with child waiting for her time, counting the minutes of her pain.

Sometimes she dozed fitfully, and so did I, stretched out as I was on the floor near the stove. Waiting for a new life to begin is a most peculiar waiting. There is a hushed and holy quality about it. It is as if one were in church. It is both hard and sweet. It is as if one were listening with one's soul to hear God's words of command, of creation.

The pain was coming more intensely now, but still the woman was not ready. It was going to be a hard delivery. The doctor was worried. He thought he might have to take her to the hospital. In any case, this house was too small for the kind of operation he had in mind.

He decided that she would have to get up and walk the mile or more to the place where he had left the car. If he could get the car moving (perhaps a neighbor had already succeeded in doing this for him) he might reach the hospital in time. If not, well, there was a larger house near the car. Perhaps the operation could be performed there.

We got the woman up and made her ready for the long walk. It was morning by now. The air was fresh and cold, most welcome after the humid atmosphere of the tiny house. The sun was peering over the hill and the birds were talking to it. We walked slowly. The doctor went on ahead with giant strides, carrying his satchel and my bag. We paused every few moments, the woman and I, because her pains were becoming greater.

O the grit of our women! The quiet courage, the rare humor! We went up the first hill with painful slowness. It began to rain on top of everything else. The woman leaned up against a boulder, racked with pain, but smiling.

I thought of immaculate white hospitals, and of rich, pampered women surrounded by nurses and doctors. I thought of women who were streamlined, painted and slim, who feared their children's birth mostly because of what it would do to their figures!

"This will be my 10th baby," the woman said. She said it not exactly with pride but certainly with joy. She mentioned her first nine trials, trying to distract herself from the present waves of pain that shook her. We went slowly on.

"I can remember my mother telling me about women who had their children in the fields," she said. "One of mine I had all by myself. My goodness I was scared! I remembered only the one thing that I *must* do: the doctor said that I must boil the scissors. They are still rusty!"

We rested again and she told me of the children who had

died and of her children who had lived. In her face was a light, a glow that could not have been captured by any artist's brush. It was like the shadow of God's face. I shivered a little from sheer awe.

The doctor was by now far ahead. We couldn't even see him. "It doesn't matter," the woman said with a brave grin. "He has the instruments but we have the baby clothes—and the baby—the most important things!"

I asked our Lady to let us at least reach the neighbor's house if we could not make it in time to the hospital. The doctor had thought that the walk might shorten the woman's time, and might also make the operation easier both for him and the woman. He was right. The child would soon be born now, perhaps before we were even halfway to the car.

We kept on walking, slowly, resting. We reached the car. But the pain was already too great. Somehow we got her to the neighbor's house. Water was boiled, the instruments were sterilized and everyone went desperately to work —and to prayer.

The silence was broken only by the crackle of the fire, the whisper of the doctor's voice, and the groans of the woman. And then—wonder of wonders!—the cry of a new-born baby. The first cry of the baby merged with the last cry of the mother, and a man was born. Alleluia!

The sun outside was now warm. The birds sang. The trees showed new, lovely green shades. A collie barked at the team pulling the doctor's car out of the mud. Before long we were off, riding through the scented pines, back to the waiting Blue Door.

I climbed back into my bed that I had left so many hours before. I slept, this time without dreams, to await the next call for help that most surely would come through the Blue Door.

Karl Stern

I forget exactly where I met Karl Stern for the first time—the man who wrote *The Flight from Woman, Pillar of Fire, The Third Revolution, Through Dooms of Love.* In musical circles he was known as an outstanding musician who became a psychiatrist; in psychiatric circles he was known as an outstanding psychiatrist who was also an outstanding musician!

One thing is certain, Dr. Karl Stern passed many times through the Blue Door of Madonna House in Combermere. It was always a benediction to have him come. He didn't sit yoga fashion like Bob Lax. He sat on an ordinary piano stool and played our old piano that I had purchased 40 years ago or more for Friendship House in Toronto. Under his fingers the piano sang. Somehow it filled our loneliness. It consoled us. It made us weep and laugh, and it brought us peace.

He told us about the books he had written and about the ones he was writing now. He told us stories about his patients, stories that also helped us and gave us courage. I remember one of them especially.

We had been talking about the terrible mental sickness of anxiety, and we ventured to say that Christ must have been very anxious, so anxious that he sweated blood on that terrible stone in the strange garden of Gethsemani. Dr. Stern said that Christ indeed had been anxious and had sweat blood, but that he had had a patient once who also was very anxious, so anxious that he too sweated blood—probably not as profusely as Christ, but nevertheless it was there.

I sat listening to the story and thought of the anxiety of all the people all over the world. How many people are sweating blood and tears? During the Second World War Churchill told the English people that all he could offer them was blood and tears. Somehow, I don't think of sweating blood over shrapnel and bullets, but over men bowed down by terrible anxiety.

Then I thought about the God who became man for our sake. He was about to face the lifting of all the sins of mankind upon his back. No wonder he sweated blood. I wanted so much to wipe his face, to console him, to be one who hasn't slept through his agony. Then I looked at Dr. Karl Stern, and I said to myself that God has given wondrous minds to some people, and that this doctor who was telling us these stories was one of these men.

I thought too of Christ washing the feet of his apostles and wiping them with a towel, and suddenly it all became clear. God had given Karl Stern a towel of profound intelligence and the water of discernment to know when and how to wipe the faces of men and women who were sweating blood in the throes of anxiety. And in a flash I somehow understood the role of the psychiatrist—to wipe from the hearts of men the pain inflicted on them by others, inflicted by the inhumanity of man to man.

Yes, Dr. Karl Stern passed many times through the Blue Door of Madonna House. Our memories of him are like sounds of music that came from his heart to ours and brought us joy and peace.

When I think of Karl Stern, I think of him as a Christian with a towel over his arm and holding a basin of fresh, cool water. He is wiping the heart of Christ in the hearts of men. I think of him as consolation.

A Quiet Flame

The girl who walked through the Blue Door was slender and pale. Her face expressed a hunger for deep life that almost leaped out at one and begged to be satisfied. As the days passed she merged with the others in the house, going about her little chores in a quiet and simple way. She spoke little but observed much.

One evening she sat with me by the wide river and we listened to the glories of the setting sun sung in colors that beggared the imagination. Softly she spoke. She said she had a heart disease, had had it from early youth. Yet she wished to become a staff worker, a member of the inner family of Friendship House, if that were possible.

I remained silent for quite a long time. Combermere was a pioneering branch of our lay apostolate. It was very demanding physically. It was difficult also because one needed faith and vision to see here the beginning of a harvest of souls. In the beginning there were only the three of us— myself, Eddie and "Flewy"—three lonely grains of wheat in the process of dying, as grains of wheat must if they are to bring forth the harvest. Had this girl what it takes—to see and to die?

I looked up and my eyes met those eyes hungry for the Absolute. Suddenly I made up my mind that I would take her, heart condition and all. We needed her, she had much to give, and she needed us. And so it came to pass that Patricia Conners became the first staff worker of Madonna House.

Her family graciously let her go, though her mother knew how death might claim her at any time. Hers was that kind of family, centered on Christ.

Pat stayed with us for almost two years. At first, to the astonishment of all, her health improved very much. Then, slowly, she became more and more tired. Soon the tiredness grew so intense that we knew she had to leave us.

Montreal was her hometown, and Montreal, even as Combermere, felt Pat's presence. It was an intangible feeling. She was like a beautiful candle that burns straight and bright, yet much too fast. She illuminated dark places beyond the scope of an ordinary candle flame, perhaps because of the intensity with which it burned.

Pat's was a hidden intensity, peaceful, full of the immense charity of Christ that hears no evil, thinks no evil and speaks no evil. Intensity and transparency of soul—that was what Pat brought into the world. That is what she left in Madonna House. A legacy of love and light. That is what she bequeathed to her friends in Montreal too.

She passed through life as a lovely lighted candle, and left behind a shaft of light and fire that will light other fires. She was a contemplative in the marketplace. Perhaps that is why she did so much for Christ in her neighbor. Her doing was the overflowing of the chalice of herself which was always being filled with the Lord.

Though she had to leave us, she is still part of this humble lay apostolate. Pat died peacefully in her sleep one night. She joined "Flewy," one of the originals whom she loved so much, and Larry Lee, a Negro staff worker of our Washington House. These three staff workers passed through the Blue Door and have now passed through the door of eternal life. We believe that they are standing before the face of the Christ they loved and served so well on earth. "Flewy, Pat, and Larry, pray for us. You better than anyone else know our many needs."

A Member of Satan's Church

He was a nice young man. He stood outside the Blue Door at Madonna House, looking at some flowers. When I approached him he smiled and, shaking my hand warmly, asked if this really was Madonna House. I said yes, it really was Madonna House. He continued quietly (yet, watching me intently) explaining that he belonged to the Church of Satan in one of the cities of Canada, and would it be possible for him to stay with us a week.

I must admit that I was a little bit shocked inwardly. But being used to all kinds of people, and remembering our commitment to hospitality, I said it would be all right for him to stay for a week. Would he like some coffee? He consented to the latter and together we passed through the Blue Door. I prayed that our Lady would bless him with many blessings.

We sat down and had our coffee, and I inquired why he came to us if he belonged to the "opposition" as it were. He answered very genuinely that he really didn't know why he had come to Madonna House, but that some of his Christian friends told him that we were an interesting place to visit, one that he should know about. So here he was.

I tried to answer the question for him. I said that it stands to reason that if you are a worshiper of Satan you must know God. Without God Satan is a nonentity, does not exist, isn't important. I'm sure your friends sent you here so that you might get to know the God you don't know and

121

don't want to worship. By knowing God you will know Satan better, and as you know Satan better you will leave him alone faster!

We talked some more, and he stayed the whole week, watching and observing. He spoke neither about himself nor about the "church" he belonged to. Before he left he almost came to Mass, that is to say, he sat one evening on the top of the stairs which lead to the chapel. There you can hear everything and see most of what is going on.

He left after a week. As he departed he shook my hand warmly and said he would be back. He hasn't been back yet, but I think he will be. Having contacted some of his friends, I discovered that he wasn't going to his "church" anymore.

A Priest, A Man, A Woman

As the years go by, Gratitude walks with me along the road of memories. Her steps and mine are slow, and we do not talk very much. But somehow her silence speaks and makes music in my heart.

Here at Madonna House I watch the rhythm of our days slip by. I see this large family, our first branch of Friendship House in Canada, pray together and work together. My mind effortlessly crosses space and time and beholds the same rhythm in our Friendship Houses in the States many years ago.

The silence of gratitude that walks with me along the road of memories swells into a mighty song. And the song takes me back to 1938 and Harlem, New York, that city within a city, where the first Friendship House was then being established, and without which there would be no others.

I was back in my little stuffy room on 138th Street, so dark even on sunny days that you always had to have on an electric light. That many-rooms-in-one is forever etched into my very being. Kitchen, dining room, bedroom, office, the tiny hall where one could barely turn around, the small bathroom—all are there in my mind. There is also the window that opened onto a courtyard and which shut out the sky and magnified, as with a loudspeaker, all the noises of a noisy tenement, plus the strange cacophany of umpteen radios playing—each a different program!

Heat, cold, perpetual twilight, endless noise encom-

123

passed me; loneliness, fear and temptations to pack and return to the Canada I knew and loved filled my heart and soul. Sleep fled from me. The pulse beats of a restless, overcrowded Harlem that never sleeps came in and made their home with me.

I would go outside and walk the teeming streets and wonder what I, a lonely white woman from a distant land, was doing in this segregated, human sea of brown, yellow and black faces.

Sure, I was there for Love's sake, love of Christ in the Negro. But, oh, how far, far away Christ seemed! All I could see was the Negro whom I did not know, and who did not know me either or seem to want to.

It was at this time that God reminded me that I was not alone. Through the Blue Door of our library, freshly painted in honor of our Lady, he often came to visit me in three people in particular: our saintly pastor, Father Michael Mulvoy, Emmanuel Romero, and Ida MacDonald. There perhaps would never have been a Friendship House in the United States had it not been for these three.

Only those of us who have walked the long road of loneliness that is the road of the lay apostolate know what it means to have the pastor of one's parish at one's side, fully! I had such a pastor with all the depth of understanding that only priestly souls can give, with the power and blessing that only the paternity of a pastor can confer and with the charity of deep comprehension of the difficulties, trials and darkness inherent in the apostolate.

Father Michael gave me all these things. Like the true shepherd that he was, he stood over us, his "tiny flock" of pioneering lay apostles, and guarded us against all evils. Anytime, night or day I could go to him with all emergencies. And how many of these there were during the first years of travail in Friendship House only he and I and God know.

It seems that not a week passed but the Blue Door

opened to let him through. He came with blessings, advice, understanding and help of every kind. Where can I find the words with which to thank him for all these things?

And then there was Mr. Romero. He was a brilliant man, originally from Jamaica. He was a holy man, a Tertiary of St. Francis like myself and my brother in that extraordinary saint. What would I have done without his showing me, one by one, the obstacles to be overcome, the right turn to be taken at the crossroads, the way out of the labyrinth which race relations were to me. I had lived for a long time in an intellectual fog.

Of Russian-Polish origin, I had never encountered prejudice. From childhood I had associated the U.S.A. with freedom, democracy and the high ideals of government. And now I was actually and factually living in and touching Harlem, this city within a city, built on prejudice and on the denial of all that democracy stood for. It was a city of broken dreams and broken ideals.

It was a labyrinth indeed. If it hadn't been for the gentle and constant guidance of my friend and brother in St. Francis, how could I have ever remained in such a maze and stayed sane? Where do I find the words to thank *him* as well?

And Ida MacDonald. Quiet, calm, the first Negro along with Mr. Romero to have faith in the dream that I was bringing to Harlem. It was then a somewhat formless dream, one that I could not quite put into words. It had to be lived and seen to be believed.

Ida was always there when there was something to do. She was present at the birth of the Clothing Centre, the Library, the Adult Education Program, the Youth Centres and the setting up of the office. She entered books, gave out clothing, worked on filing cards way into the night. She always encouraged me, just by being there, just because she had the right word to say at the right time. Where can I find the words to thank people like this?

A priest, a man, a woman. I sing to them the silent but immense song of my gratitude. I know full well that no one can give me words to adequately thank them. So I turn to the Gracious Mother of God and beg her to do so in my stead.

The Two Nuns

This is not an ordinary story. I set it down here because it already is kind of "public property" in and around Combermere. Many of the senior members of the community know it. They would tell it to you, with a few exaggerations maybe (simply out of love for me). So, I want to tell it myself, to make sure it is remembered as simply and as near the truth as possible.

One afternoon, while I was working in the garden, in the flower bed by the river, a man came to see me. His name was George. He was a local farmer with a weather-beaten but pleasant face. He was of medium height and had piercing blue eyes and a patch of white hair. He stood silently, looking me over. I was used to this, understanding that he, like most country people, was not loquacious. At least the men aren't!

"Be you the nurse?" he asked.

I answered, "Yes, I am."

He said, "My woman is mighty sick. She's got cancer. The doctor ordered her some powerful medicine. You give it through a needle. My niece is a nurse. She was visiting us. Them needles must be given once every 24 hours. She was giving them but she had to go home. I can't get no nurse no place. What about you, Ma'am? Would you mind giving her a needle a day?"

I replied that I wouldn't mind at all. He explained that he lived on the top of a mountain and pointed directly to the peaks you can see on the horizon if you look down the river

127

from the windows of Madonna House. On the top of the highest point stands a farmhouse which you cannot distinguish too clearly because of the trees. I had never been there, but I knew it would take a long time to reach it. You had to go by a roundabout way. But I didn't ask any questions.

I laid down my hoe. I told him I was going to wash my hands and change my dress and that I would be with him in 10 minutes. But evidently he had something more to say, for he stood there, perplexed. I waited. Slowly, somewhat reluctantly, he asked, "You be a Catholic?" I said that I was. He said, "You mind that we are Protestant Orangemen?" I said that I didn't mind at all.

When I gave him my name he nodded, evidently pleased. He smiled for the first time and said that he would be waiting for me in his car.

He had a good car for our roads, a Model T Lizzy of ancient vintage. So off we went. After traveling for some time we turned sharply to the left after crossing over a bridge. We traveled up what was more a path than a road.

Up, up we climbed, through really wild country along this road. It had been a lumber road, made for the skidding of logs in the wintertime. It was rough riding, believe me. Finally, we came to a lovely farm, one that could literally be described as from "the good old days." Old-fashioned and tidy looking, it had a breathtaking view of the river.

His wife was in a room upstairs. I read the doctor's notes which he had left for the nurse. She was cancer-ridden. The fatal signs were in her intestines and in part of the alimentary canal. The doctor had prescribed for her the highest dosage of morphine I have ever seen prescribed for a patient.

I made her comfortable and gave her the hypo. I then visited a little, consoled her the best I could, and left. One of the daughters could do the bedside nursing and look after the house. As far as the food was concerned, the woman could only take small sips of water, and barely that. Occasionally she could suck a little piece of ice.

Nearly all that summer, once a day, George and I traveled to their farm. He had to make a double trip because he had to come for me and bring me back again. It was 3.9 miles from our house to his.

For about two and a half months every day, including Sundays, I made this trip with George. Around the middle of August George stopped coming. He was absent for several days. I presumed that his niece had returned and that he didn't need me anymore.

Then one morning fairly early he walked into the kitchen where I was cooking, sat down and bade me good morning. He looked troubled and frightened.

"Ma'am," he said, "I want you to phone them Sisters. My woman wants them back. I'll pay for the call."

I didn't understand. Here was an Orangeman who never had very much to do with Catholics, asking for "them Sisters." What Sisters? Orangemen would cross a street to avoid meeting a nun if they saw one coming toward them. Such a man should be talking to me about Sisters! And how in heaven's name could any nun get into that back bush? This was utterly fantastic. Had George been dreaming?

I asked George a few questions. He couldn't answer coherently, but he tried hard to explain.

He had been milking, he said, and had been late with his chores. It was past seven o'clock when he finally got to the house for supper. He found his daughter Ella in the kitchen quite perturbed. She said she had gone upstairs and found her mother looking fairly well from what she could see through the door—but it seemed that her mother was talking to two nuns! They had their backs to Ella. She would have gone in, she said, but Mom looked so happy that she didn't want to intrude.

George asked Ella how the nuns got there. He hadn't seen or heard any car. Ella said she hadn't seen or heard a car either, but she had been very busy. Perhaps someone brought them. Maybe the Catholic nurse (that's me) had brought them. George didn't go upstairs to see his wife. He was too scared or shy or something. They both decided to stay in the kitchen until the Sisters came down.

Because of his wife's sickness, George usually slept downstairs in the kitchen on a cot. They waited a long time but nothing happened. The nuns did not come down. Ella stole quietly and furtively upstairs to her own room. George laid down on his cot. They both went to sleep.

Around 4 a.m., or maybe 5, George couldn't remember exactly, Ella woke him. Mom was calling him. He went upstairs on the double. His wife told him, with face shining, that she had had a wonderful night. She said that from the time those nuns had come to see her, all her pains had left her. She felt especially good when the young one had held her hand. She said they didn't talk much. She was so happy to be without pain that she didn't know what to say.

The young one stayed near her. The older one remained in the rocking chair. The young nun simply sat on her bed and held her hand. She was a powerfully good person. She took the pain away. Now she felt fine. She wanted a strong cup of tea—with cream! She wanted to be washed. She wanted a new nightgown.

George said he kept looking at his wife with her new shining face, wondering. Evidently she was still, even now, without pain. He told Ella to do what Mother wanted.

Ella was bewildered. She could barely move her mother, even to give her a bedbath as I had instructed her to do. It always took such a long time. She had to be so careful with Mom. She had to rub her bedsores with alcohol, and her mother had not been able to take any nourishment, not even tea. Mom hadn't been able to keep anything in her stomach except water and ice. And now tea! A bath! A new nightgown!

Ella obeyed. And goodness gracious, her mother even turned herself around a couple of times! When the bath was finished Ella put her in a clean nightgown and watched her slowly drink her tea. She actually relished it. Most amazing of all, the tea stayed down. She had another cup about noon. During all that day, Mom had a good sleep and no pain. She slept well again that night—and still no pain.

About seven o'clock this morning the pains had returned and the mother had sent George to me post haste "to get them nuns back, even if she had to pay them!"

Who were the nuns? How did they get in there? Who sent them? What did they look like? What sort of habit did they have on? George said they wore a rough brown thing with a black, narrow apron that started somewhere around their necks. Anyhow, that's how his woman described them. They had soft white collars of some sort around their necks. They had something over their heads so you couldn't see their hair. And over the white thing they had black veils. (Was George describing the Carmelites?) They had no stockings, he said. They had sandals on their bare feet.

All of a sudden as George was speaking, I didn't feel too well! The kitchen was going around and around in a peculiar way. The woman said that both nuns were good-looking. The older one was the most beautiful woman she had ever seen. The young one had black or brown eyes, a round face, and a soft voice.

I wished the kitchen would stop spinning! As close as I could make out, the Little Flower had appeared to this woman! The Little Flower and Our Lady of the Visitation were my nursing patron saints. I always took Our Lady of the Visitation with me when I went to help a patient, and I also usually left the Little Flower as the night nurse. And all this from an Orangeman who once thought Catholic nuns were the stepchildren of Satan!

I got up and walked around to prove to myself that I

was awake and that this was actually what George was saying. I set myself the task of telling George that I couldn't "phone" those nuns. Let me put it this way: I tried hard not to imply that this whole thing was a bit unusual. I think he got the gist of it. He became very pensive. Then he said simply, "The woman was always a good one. Maybe God sent them nuns." That was as close as we came to an agreement. But, he was still reluctant to leave without them. He wanted to know if there wasn't some way I could get them to come back.

I said, "George, do you believe in the Mother of our Lord? Do you like her, do you believe that she is powerful enough to help us?"

His answer was typical. "Sure I do. The Mother of the Lord is an admirable woman, powerful too, I guess."

That was a good beginning for an Orangeman. I had some medals of our Lady, blessed by the pope. I asked him if he would mind giving one to his wife. I said it would be nice for her to have it. Mary was better than any nun. Mary was a woman, and she would understand. Her picture would help in many, many ways.

Strangely enough, he didn't refuse the medal. He said he would take it because of me and "because of them nuns."

I didn't see him then for quite a while. Two weeks later he returned. His wife had died. He said that when he returned with the medal but without the nuns, his wife had not been distressed about it. He was happy to see her put the medal on her nightdress. Half an hour later she went to sleep. Her pains had vanished. She woke up in the middle of the night and called for him.

Being an inarticulate man, he did not express himself very well, but in a few words he gave me a beautiful picture of a husband and wife who had loved each other very much and who were now having one last intimate talk together.

She wanted to be propped up so that her head rested on his shoulder. She wanted him to hold her tightly against him. She felt a great strength; she could then sit up a little.

Together they went over their life and thanked God for the good years they had known. "It was like we just got married," he said. "We both felt that way." After a while she nestled closer and kissed him. She asked him to kiss her back and to put her head on his shoulder. He thought that she then fell asleep, but she had died.

Death by cancer seldom occurs like that. The pains usually increase to an incredible pitch and the patients are usually given a greater dosage of morphine.

He had her buried with the medal, Orangeman or no Orangeman. He said he hadn't asked me to the funeral because he knew I was busy, but that some of the last words of his wife were words of gratitude to me, gratitude, love and friendship.

Such is the story I wanted to tell you. I make no comments or draw any conclusions. I just wanted to relate the facts. But the story has a funny sequel.

George was a popular person in his village. In his loneliness he started visiting the local club which every general store was apt to have. There he would tell his story—and the story grew!

The next I heard about it was when people started coming to me from that village, asking for "healing tokens." I had a hard time convincing them that I didn't have such "tokens." Then, one day, the parish priest called me to his rectory. He didn't look too happy. He wanted to know about the story which was going around that I had miraculous powers of healing. I laughed out loud and proceeded to tell him the story just as I have told it to you. He was thoughtful for a while and then he said, "Well, let's let it rest the way it is."

III

Stories of Eternity

The How Stories

Some time ago an abbot of a contemplative monastery wrote and asked me if I would temporarily accept one of his monks. This monk was suffering from epilepsy and the doctor had recommended a different environment for a while. Of course we gladly accepted.

Very soon a tall, strong-looking man arrived. He was very silent, and yet he was also lots of fun. Somehow the two went together. He had a few fits while he was with us, and I nursed him during his six-month stay.

Often, after one of his fits, as he was resting, he would say to me, "Tell me a story." So, on the spot, I made up a story. Halfway through it he would usually begin to fall asleep. By the time I finished it he would be fast asleep. I became adept at timing the stories to that exact moment. And that's how the *How Stories* came into being.

How Death Became Life

Death was born on a flaming day—at least that was the way she remembered it. For when she came forth, full-grown into the world, it was alight with all the colors of fire. The light seemed to come from a sword which an immense angel held aloft, guarding a door that led she knew not where.

At first, Death felt like a stranger on earth. She wandered around kind of lost. Then, one day, she saw a beautiful bird with snowy white plumage. Gently she walked up to it and stretched out her hand to feel the softness of its feathers which shone so brightly in the sun.

No sooner had her fingers touched it than the bird fell at her feet, cold and still. Death picked it up, wondering why it had stopped singing and stopped living. And that was how she discovered her dreaded power, and then she understood why she had been born on a flaming day.

Slowly, the years flowed into eternity where all time goes. Death traveled through them all, touching now this animal, now that bird, this fish or that flower. By then she knew the whole earth very well. She had also noticed that a creature called Man dwelt on it, who still held in his face a strange reflection of God. It was as though he had been made in the image of God.

Death took a long time to touch Man. But one day she did—and she saw him shudder. He cried out and became as cold and as still as that first white bird. On that day Death tasted the fullness of her awesome power. But also on that day she knew loneliness to its very last bitter drop.

From then on, as the centuries turned into thousands of years and the thousands turned into millions, Death claimed all living things for her own. Yet, there was in her a hunger that grew. In her silent kingdom nothing remained. All living things crumbled and turned into dust at her touch. She was always left alone with loneliness. There were days—years even—when Death went almost mad with loneliness, mad with the desire to have and to hold something that would last, something or someone that she could call her own.

It was now a time of great plagues, storms and floods. With tears flowing down her emaciated cheeks Death criss-crossed the whole earth with the swiftness born of her frenzied hunger. Throwing herself at the children of men, she embraced them passionately, hoping against hope that she might hear a word or see a smile that would lift the pall of loneliness that isolated her from all living things and held her tighter, always tighter.

Men feared Death above all things. They shrank from her approach. They invented thousands of legends about her being incapable of really harming them. They imagined a life after Death's touch which would somehow resemble the earthly life they were used to.

Slowly these legends grew into religions and beliefs centered on ways and means of escaping Death's clammy embrace. Their attempts left a wide trail of religious artifacts scattered all over the earth. Other men dig in earth's bowels just to see this trail.

But Death kept walking the earth. At times she smiled at men's fear of her and subtly enjoyed her power over them. At other times she wept bitterly, not only because she was so lonely, but also because she sensed that some unknown part of man always seemed to escape her.

One day, tired and weary, she sat on a hill beneath three crosses on which three men were being executed. She

did not feel like looking at or touching any one of these. She
was too tired, too lonely, too disconsolate. So she just sat
there with her weary head in her hands and wept slow, huge
tears, bemoaning her aloneness.

Suddenly she heard a voice say softly, "I thirst." She
looked up. Her gaze met two fathomless eyes. From their
depths flowed a brilliant, warm, blue light, the likes of which
she had never experienced before.

Instantly she stood up, rigid, erect, tall and thin. A few
paces away hung this Man between the two others. She
somehow did not dare to touch him, though she wanted to
more than she had ever wanted to touch anything or anybody.

Very self-consciously she put her hands behind her back
and stared at his bleeding and disfigured face as if she could
never see enough. She heard him speak some more short little
sentences. Each word she locked in her heart. She relished
them. The very echo of his voice, weak with pain and sorrow,
moved her deeply.

Then he was silent, but his eyes called to her in a word-
less message. She did not know how it happened, but gently,
oh, ever so gently, she touched his cheek. He seemed, for an
instant, to smile for her alone. Then like all the others before
him, he closed his eyes and became lifeless and cold!

She could not believe it! Somehow she knew without
knowing that he was different from all the others. So she
lingered for a while. She saw him taken down from the cross.
She saw his mother hold his lifeless body in her arms and
cradle his ashen face against her bosom. She saw him carried
into a tomb in the hollow of a cave. She saw some soldiers
roll a heavy stone in front of the entrance to seal it.

Then, fleet of foot and noiseless as only Death can be,
she entered the cave just before the stone was put in place.
What passed there between him and Death no human being
will ever know. One thing is certain. On the following Sunday, two days after he had been taken down from the cross,

some women came to the tomb and it was empty. Death was not there.

Since that Sunday morning, all those who look upon Death with the eyes of faith in that Man see Death differently. Now she is beautiful. They know that her touch brings life, not death. Now Death is God's messenger of love to men. Love is life, and Death is now the loving gate to everlasting life, herself alive.

How Reason Became Mature

Reason came to dwell on earth with the creation of Man. There was about her then a beauty and grace that was a joy to behold. But something strange happened to her after Man was sent out of paradise to earn his bread in the sweat of his brow.

Her childlike simplicity slowly became more and more complex. Her gracious transparency became clouded. Her submissiveness disappeared and she began to assert herself in many strange ways. She began preening herself and taking on airs that she never had before. Somewhat haughtily, she guided Man's footsteps and advised and directed him in his endeavors.

As centuries flowed into centuries, Reason beheld the works of her hands, found them good, and grew more and more proud of herself. In fact, she began to consider herself as the "heart of the matter." When Man began to worship her as if she were a god in her own right, when temples were erected and special honors given to men whom Reason had especially favored, she took all these marks of respect, adulation and worship as her strict due.

Time seemed to add stature to Reason. Austere, cold, ascetic-looking, Reason walked with slow, measured, majestic tread. She was always unhurried, always full of her own importance, always walking as royalty walks at some official procession. Once in a while throughout the endless centuries, she paused and held court. Her throne was of green jade.

It offset her somber flowing garments to perfection.

Reason never allowed Feelings, Warmth, Emotions, or Gaiety to attend her. Wherever she went, whenever she spoke to Man, only Worldly Prudence, Cold Logic and Slow Deliberation were in her retinue. She never slept, for she was firmly convinced that, should she do so, the world of Man would perish. Wasn't it obvious that she alone kept it in order? If she slept, Chaos, her sworn enemy, would take possession of the minds of men.

One day, without overmuch hurry, she was making her way to Jerusalem in Palestine, a city she liked. She was always received there with due respect. Obeisance was given her by some of the most important men who lived there. They followed her teaching almost to perfection, with that unemotional coldness that she had demanded of all her disciples.

But this time Jerusalem was different. It was all stirred up. Its inhabitants were clustering around a seemingly extraordinary Man. His face was gentle and kind, yet he commanded respect at the mere sight.

Reason paused, slightly annoyed at the delay in her usual routine. Prudence, Logic, and Deliberation paused with her. The four sat down on the lovely parapet that bordered the Temple stairs. They settled down to listen to what the regal Man in the humble dress of a Galilean had to say.

He was speaking gently, clearly, so that all could understand. He spoke of the meek inheriting the earth! He said that those who were poor in spirit were truly blessed! He said that the merciful would receive mercy! He was not making any sense at all!

Reason shuddered at such seeming unreasonableness. Logic was confused. Prudence became frightened. Deliberation was in a dither!

The Man and the crowd moved on. Throughout the following days Reason met him and the crowds followed him everywhere. He bothered her, he baffled her. He spoke as one having authority, as one who knew. Moreover, it appeared to her that he was taking the minds of men away from her! That would never do. If men really began to live according to his teachings, things would be pretty *unreasonable* all round.

Something must be done, but definitely. She went to the Pharisees and Sadducees who always had been devoted to her and listened to what they had to say. They seemed "reasonable" enough. For they were planning to put the Man to death before he aroused the whole world. This was both reasonable and logical. Yet, Reason was not satisfied. Something intangible, something important was missing from their arguments, something she could not fathom at the moment.

Restlessly she went out into the night. For once she was unattended. She wandered through the streets aimlessly until she came upon a house where the light was still on in an upper room. Entering noiselessly, she sat down in a dark corner to watch the proceedings and to listen.

There was the Man again, and his small band of a dozen or so friends. What was he doing? He was breaking some bread, blessing it and giving it to them to eat. She saw him bless wine also. She heard him say: "I give you a new commandment. Love one another as I have loved you."

Love! That sentimental, unreasonable, imprudent, illogical, emotional word! Reason had always disliked it so much. Somehow, though, it sounded quite different when he said it. Now, before her very eyes, Love became immense—a light, a fire that once kindled could change the face of the earth. Now it appeared to be greater than Reason herself.

But that was impossible! Was not she, Reason herself, the greatest thing on earth? And under heaven?

She hurried away. She was disturbed. This was a new sensation for her, she who was always in perfect possession of all her faculties. She ran, forgetting for a moment that she was royalty. She fled through the sleeping countryside.

She did not return to Jerusalem until a few days later. She paid little attention to the surroundings but was startled to hear the growing murmur of an advancing mob. She stood aside to let whoever was coming pass.

The first person to come around the corner was the Man. This time he did not look very majestic. He looked spent, wounded, dirty and tired to the point of exhaustion. On his shoulder was a huge wooden cross, the weight of which was making him stagger.

A woman was waiting for him. When he saw her he stopped for a second or two. Their eyes met, the eyes of a mother and son.

Reason fell asleep right then and there. For she had beheld Love—utter, pure, perfect Love. It was a Love giving itself for others. A Love that was loving unto death.

At that instant Reason understood that she had been created to lead men to Love, which was not *something* but *Someone*—God himself! She understood too that the Man who had baffled her with his presence and words was the Son of God. She realized that she was to be his servant, his tool to bring men to love him. She realized that from then on she would have to fall asleep at times and let Love take men through the darkness of faith, through the "cloud of unknowing," where he dwelt in such a special way. Love reigned supreme there and had no use for her.

Ever since that moment, Reason, when she has brought a person to the gates of Love, the Love that is above her, curls up and goes happily to sleep. She awakes renewed and more keen than ever. She is content now to be Man's servant and not his god. She has matured.

How Lady Avarice
Became Lady Bountiful

Lady Avarice was born old, or so it seemed to her. She could never remember the time when she was young and carefree and walked with the easy, springy step of youth. For that matter, no one else on earth could remember her young, either.

Always she had seemed to men to be slow of gait. Her thin, bony frame was almost hunchbacked from the odd way she shuffled along. She was always looking down onto the roads which she traversed so endlessly, as if she did not want to miss one inch of her way. She scrutinized each and every step, seeking something to pick up, something to hold and press tightly to her flat bosom. When she did find something she never let go of it, except to hide it someday, somewhere, in one of the many places she alone knew. She visited these places often, and from them she would emerge, only to continue her shuffle through hundreds of other years and down thousands of other roads, seeking, ever seeking more things to pick up and hoard.

If anyone had ever had time to look at Lady Avarice, he might have detected here and there slight traces of beauty. Her hair was long, the color of ashes when fire makes them glow with the glow of pale gold. But, because her hands were always full of possessions, she could not comb her hair very well. So it hung in untidy and matted strands, often covering her face and thus hiding it. Her features were regular but emaciated because, driven by that strange inner fire to always gather more and more things, she had no time to eat or drink or take care of herself.

Her eyes were really a beautiful violet, with dark, long lashes. But few people ever saw her eyes since they were always cast down in search of treasures. Those who did look into them never remembered their color, for when Lady Avarice lifted her face to gaze into the faces of men, it was only because she desired to possess their souls. And who, endangered of becoming a slave of Lady Avarice, would remember the color of her eyes?

When the fire of her ugly passion had seared a human heart, it, in turn, thought only of more and more possessions for possession's sake. All else was wiped out from the memory of those who looked into her eyes.

Outwardly, men enslaved by her appeared to be prospering. They waxed rich, and other men bowed low before them in fear and trembling. But her touch or glance seemed to change those she chose to become her own. They withered and shrank inwardly. They became bent and crooked—like her—and in their eyes burned that same unholy hunger for possessions.

These people seemed to be living, yet somehow they were dead. That is why from the dawn of creation men were afraid of Lady Avarice. They made wide detours when they saw her coming, or they quickly shut the doors of their hearts at her approach. Most men did but, alas, not all!

Some, driven by curiosity, the desire for wealth, or by their presumption in their ability to resist her, allowed her to gaze upon them. Then they were caught: they steadily looked back at her. They saw indeed the color of her eyes, but they saw much more. They saw her thin, claw-like hands stretch out and embrace them in a deadly embrace that would never again let them go.

As time went on they lost their way and were set apart from other men in the vast domains and hiding places of

Lady Avarice. They too became part of her endless possessions!

Thus it had been from the beginning of time, and thus it went on for endless centuries.

And then, one day, Time brought Lady Avarice to Palestine, to the village of Bethlehem, and to a stable where a woman was giving birth to her first child. Three Kings from the East were there, kneeling before the child's crib, offering him frankincense, myrrh and gold.

Lady Avarice, of course, could see only the gold. There was a lot of it. Coins newly minted, all shiny and beautiful as only gold can be. So beautiful was this sight to Lady Avarice that, to get a better look, she straightened her bent-over frame. At that moment she dropped the other things she was holding and stretched out her hands toward that lifeless but beautiful gold.

It was then that Mary, the Child's mother, arose. Gently she picked up her Child. Slowly, gracefully, silently, majestically, she placed him in the outstretched arms of Lady Avarice!

Lady Avarice stood perfectly still. She seemed to grow taller and even more beautiful. The Child reached out and caught a strand of her ash-gold hair. He smiled and tugged at it. And lo, the hair became untangled and flowed down and covered Lady Avarice with a mantle of surpassing beauty.

The Child laughed, and touched the eyes of Lady Avarice. Their fixed, ugly, hungry look became soft and radiant. It seemed as if they had lost themselves in the eyes of the Infant.

Suddenly, Lady Avarice bent down and kissed the Child. Then, handing him back to Mary, she sped away into the drowsy, sunlit afternoon.

No one saw her for a long time. Some who had looked into her eyes and had become her slaves appeared to be more free. They began to detach themselves from their possessions and to share them with those who were in need. But of Lady Avarice herself there was no trace.

Time, who knows so many things which are hidden from the eyes of men, knew where she was and what she was doing. She was gathering all the things she had hidden throughout the eons and loading them onto a caravan. It was a caravan the like of which earth had never seen!

When she had finished all her packing and loading, Lady Avarice and her caravan moved back across the world to Bethlehem and to the stable that was by now empty and in ruins. The family she was seeking had left it long ago. For a long time she stood in front of it, looking at the strange light that seemed to stream from it. She was the only one who saw it. Then, sadly, she turned away and walked forlornly down the wide caravan road that led to Jerusalem.

She and her treasure-laden camels wound their ghostly way through the city and on out the other side. As she approached the hill of Golgotha she saw three crosses on top, and a man affixed to each.

It was before the man in the middle that Lady Avarice stopped. Lifting her face she looked at him long and hard. But she could not in her imagination recapture the face of the Child in the face of the dying Man.

Then her eyes fell on the face of Mary, his mother, who stood beneath his cross. Now Lady Avarice knew! She fell weeping at the feet of Mary. Then, calling to her caravan, she had all her treasures laid at Mary's feet.

But Mary shook her head. She bade Lady Avarice to be truly generous with her treasures and to give them to those most in need—and to give in the name of her son, Jesus.

From that day onward, Lady Avarice changed her name and became Lady Bountiful, the servant of Lady Charity. She became one searching always for more to give and not to hoard.

True, Avarice still finds a home in the hearts of some

men. But it is not Lady Avarice anymore; it is a phantom, a ghost brought forth from the depths of hell to confuse and bewilder men.

Whenever Lady Bountiful, the servant of Lady Charity, meets her ghostlike past in the hearts of men, she slays it by telling the story of a Child's kiss.

How Pity Returned to Love

One day Lady Pity awoke quite confused. Of course, it did not happen all at once—the confusion that is. It had started long ago. But this particular morning it really made her wonder. It made her decide that something just had to be done about it, and that it had to be done *now*.

The crux of the whole problem was her place in the order of things. Up to a certain time (she could not remember exactly when) she had been content to be in attendance on Lady Charity whose other name was Love. She had been satisfied to be one of the many, for Love had many other attendants besides Pity. Understanding, Gentleness, Kindness, Forgiveness, Humility, Knowledge—Lady Pity had been part of this entourage for more eons than she cared to remember.

Then, one day (she had lost track of time), it occurred to her that she was quite an important personage in her own right. So, instead of being simply one among many in the retinue of Lady Charity, she should really have a retinue of her own, or, at least, be "on her own" as all important personages are.

At first, this was a rather startling idea. She rejected it as unseemly. But the notion kept coming back, coming back, in spite of all she did to get rid of it. She really had tried to get rid of it for many centuries. But the idea would not let her go. It brought her more and more confusion until this day when she awoke thoroughly confused.

By noon of that fateful day she had decided to act. This was very foolish of her. One should never act when one is confused. But Lady Pity did. That evening she just quietly walked away from Love.

Lady Pity had never been alone before and did not know where to go. So, she went straight ahead! As she walked slowly through the starry night she made her plans. Of course! She knew what to do! She would just be herself! Men had need of Pity ever since the first man had been thrown out of paradise. But men needed Pity even more since that extraordinary Man (who, she eventually learned, was the Son of God) had come to earth. His heart and eyes were so full of Love and Pity that men, having caught her reflection in his eyes—needed her now more than ever.

It was simple. Now that she was so important and "on her own," she would go and help men everywhere. By and by she would get the recognition that she so well deserved. She would acquire a retinue of her own and reveal to all the truly important personage she really is. Thus ran her thoughts.

She walked faster and with more firm steps now. And that is when she came upon the young man and woman sitting on a park bench talking. Something in the posture of the young woman caught Lady Pity's eye. The woman seemed dejected. She was crying, as if to herself. Pity came nearer and noticed that the man was talking somewhat harshly. This would never do, thought Pity. She sat quite close to him. He looked up into her face. Though he could not see her with his bodily eyes, he felt her presence. His voice changed pitch. It became filled with Pity.

Lady Pity smiled to herself, proud of her power over men!

Then, a strange thing happened. The girl stopped crying. She lifted a bewildered, hurt face to the man. She told him that she did not want pity without love! With that she rose and walked, nay ran, away from him. He shrugged his broad shoulders, shook his head, lit a cigarette and walked away. He left Pity sitting on the bench, lost in consternation at what could have possibly gone wrong.

After a while Lady Pity rose and, her problem still unsolved, moved on. In due time she came to a big city. Wandering through it she came to the poorest section. She noticed a well-dressed woman, laden with all kinds of gifts, going about from house to house. Feeling that she might help, Pity followed her.

They went into home after home, the woman with the gifts and Lady Pity. They were poor homes, almost destitute, where the woman was received courteously enough but with a strange lack of warmth. Tired mothers with kids hiding in their skirts smiled dead smiles. They meekly accepted the gifts and listened to words filled with Pity. But they said little beyond a perfunctory "Thank you."

Astonished, Pity stayed on in one of the homes after the lady with the gifts had left. Once more she heard strange words, words about the bitterness of receiving alms given out of sheer pity without love.

Lady Pity refused to believe what she was hearing, but as she walked up and down throughout the whole world year after year she became discouraged. She went into a church to think things over. In the vanishing twilight a statue drew her gaze. She was startled to recognize the God-Man she had once met in her endless pilgrimages when she was an attendant to Love. It seemed that his eyes looked at her with deep Pity, but it was a clear, transparent Pity that received all its beauty from Love.

At that moment Pity understood that, alone, without Love, she could not help anyone. She understood that she was an attendant in the retinue of Love, and Love was more than Pity could ever be. Love, after all, was a Person, was God. Love alone could make Pity warm, friendly and healing. Without Love she was a dead and lifeless thing.

That very night Pity came back where she belonged. She came back to Love.

How Sorrow Became Joyful

Sorrow was born of a man and a woman when, turning their faces away from the gates of paradise which had been closed to them by the Almighty, they made their way slowly into the grayness of the immense and lonely earth. Sorrow walked along with them.

Sorrow did not remember her birthday. She thought she had always been here on our earth. She did not realize her age either. She herself never changed. She was slender and not very tall. She never hurried, always moved slowly as if she were dead tired.

She had deep, violet eyes which had the power to pierce the hearts of those she looked at. She was graceful, in a quiet way. Her blue-black hair was beautifully cared for and always tied with ribbons that matched the color of her eyes. Her flowing garments were of the same color. No matter what kind of day it was, the hues in it were always violet, which fit in better with the purples of night than the sun of the day.

Lady Sorrow was definitely a person of moods. Now she would seek solitude, now crowds of people. One thing was certain: Every man born of woman knew her slow, rhythmical step, and felt the heaviness that at times bowed people almost to the ground. Sometimes it even brought them to the very brink of despair. This was caused by her glance, sometimes brushing men slightly, sometimes lingering on their faces for what seemed to them an eternity.

Now and then Lady Sorrow would attach herself to

especially one person. It might be a man, a woman, a child, a maiden, some old person who was almost blind. It seemed that even people who were really blind could feel and see the effects of Sorrow's steady gaze. No one ever entirely escaped her in the course of the journey from one eternity to the other.

Often Sorrow wondered at the effect she had on people. She was very lonely for she knew that she was not welcomed by anyone. As far back as she could remember they did a thousand strange things to get rid of her. At times, in her solitude, she was herself beset by the memories of gods they prayed to, of the incantations they kept up through many long nights and days, of the endless rituals they engaged in—all to get rid of her and the effects of her deeply shadowed, violet eyes.

There were moments when she would flee to her solitudes, which was not very sensible. It was not very sensible because when Lady Sorrow felt sorry for herself, she could not act at all sensibly.

Time, which for her had no meaning, marched on. In fact, as year after year passed, she ceased to take any notice of Time at all. Yet she was restless.

It was during one such restless day that she left her solitude in the desert and wandered slowly toward the homes of men. On the fringe of the desert she stopped, startled. There was a Man being attended to by angels—beautiful, translucent spirits. They hovered round about him, lovingly yet reverently.

Sorrow could not move. An odd thing happened to her. She lowered her gaze and covered her eyes. Her long, dark lashes cast a shadow on her thin cheeks. It seemed that, for the first time, she did not want to look into a man's eyes.

He called her to him. She thrilled at the sound of his voice. It seemed that the very essence of music was contained in it—no, that it had had its *birth* in him. She hesitated for just a fraction of a second, and then slowly, shyly, she approached, her eyes still downcast.

He was speaking again, and again the music of his voice enveloped her and lifted her up, up, into regions she never knew existed. This time he bade her look at him. She did not want to. She realized that her glance brought sadness, pain and darkness, and she did not want to give him any of those things.

She wished she could give him laughter, joy and gladness! But then, he had them all already, for that was what was hidden in the music of his voice.

She looked up. Their eyes met. He smiled, as if he had been waiting a long, long time for just this meeting. It's as if he knew it would take place here and now, and he was glad it had.

Bewildered, unsure of herself, Lady Sorrow just stood there unable to tear her gaze from his. Afterwards, she would never be able to tell anyone their color. All she saw in them was glory, glory the likes of which she had not dreamed existed.

He stretched out his hand and beckoned her to sit down beside him. Obediently, like a child, she complied. The hovering angels formed a ring around them and, bowing their heads, softly chanted adoring songs.

He began to speak. She listened. No one except he and she and the angels ever heard what passed between them. It was night when they parted. But from that day until now she became his shadow, and followed him wherever he went. She only left him to go to Mary, his mother. Then came the day he was to die.

Just before he died their eyes met—his from the height of the cross, hers from below, next to his mother. Whatever his glance told her, she understood, and locked it in her heart forever. Since that day she has never been the same. Yes, she still walks the earth and lives with men. Yes, her glance still brings them loneliness and pain and darkness. But if they have courage she leads them now, lovingly and gently, into the Kingdom of that Man. It is a Kingdom of peace and joy which no one can take away, not even Sorrow.

After that day Sorrow knew when she was born and why. She discovered that she was born to lead men through her paths to the paradise that they lost and which was restored to them by the Man whom the angels fed in the desert.

How Pride Became Humble

Lady Pride was born proud. She never remembered a time when she had not been filled with an overwhelming admiration for herself. She passed through the ages with the arrogance of people who are sure that they are better, more clever and in every way superior to others. She always held her beautiful head very high, and she walked slowly, majestically across the centuries.

She did not bother to deal with all men to the same degree. While she influenced all, she chose her select company very carefully. If she liked someone she would come and stay with him for a long, long time, and everyone would soon see her influence. People imitated her quite well. They, like her, became cold, aloof and unapproachable, behaving as if they were set apart somehow above the common lot of humans.

She was quite beautiful, despite her disposition! Her beauty could not be denied. She was tall and stately, with features that could be called "classical" by those who know about such things. Yet, men, by and large, were afraid of her and of her beauty. There was something about it that was evil, dark and sinister. It reminded them of deep, still, stagnant waters, greenish in color, that could not sustain but only killed life. All living things died in such waters.

Anyone who has traveled can observe the desolate landscapes created by such waters. Gray, lifeless trees lift their leafless arms to heaven as if crying out of some strange depths. The shores are bereft of flowers or grass, covered only with sand and rocks. Water flowers refuse to take root. Such waters are dead—dead and frightening.

It is of such scenes that men thought whenever they saw Lady Pride pass by. They shivered and turned away. Yet, they knew that she often showered her gifts upon her friends. Gold and silver seemed to be hers to give. Power followed in her wake, a slave to her whims. But it was a darksome power, and it only served her and her friends.

Lady Pride often recalled her many conquests, but in one event she took an especial pride. It had happened long, long ago, perhaps on or near the day she was born. It had been an extraordinary day, for she never remembered ever having been young, on that day or any other. She had been born mature. It was the day on which God—he who is— had revealed his secret to the angels. After he had revealed it to them they were all enthralled, and they remained very, very still.

Lady Pride had not heard the secret, but she saw one beautiful spirit, who seemed to be all light, frown. He was so beautiful that she desired to be with him forever. She walked softly over to him and whispered to him that, whatever the secret was, it was not for him (for she saw he did not like what he heard). Why should he accept it? He was, she convinced him, as great as God himself!

The angel of light turned, saw her and believed what she said. Then, rising to an immense height, he shouted for all to hear the motto of Pride: *"Non serviam . . . I will not serve!"* Many of the lesser angels joined him after they too had looked at Lady Pride. And there ensued a battle that rocked the heavens.

For once, Lady Pride put aside her dignity. She joined in the battle on the side of Lucifer, the Angel of Light. All of a sudden, in the midst of the battle, she stood still. She beheld an awesome and frightening thing. Light was leaving the angel of light and darkness was entering into him. His beauty remained, but now it was the beauty of deadliness—a travesty of all beauty. One contact with it spelled death forever.

Immediately, he and his armies fell down, down into depths that Lady Pride never knew existed! She followed, but she could not remain in hell. She was earthly as well as hellish. As the centuries rolled on she would come back to hell now and then for a visit. Satan still fascinated her. She allowed herself to be used by him whenever he wished. Perhaps that is another reason why men were always afraid of her. Who can tell?

Maybe too, men remembered Lady Pride's part in the fall of their first parents. Naturally, she was there too, in the garden with the snake. It seemed as if her sole purpose of existence was to extend the awful domain of the angel of light who had become now the Prince of Darkness!

One starry night Lady Pride was walking, in her slow, majestic fashion, pausing now and then to admire her own reflection in the various lakes, rivers and pools that dotted her way. She found herself on the outskirts of a small village, the entrance to which was a narrow path. On both sides of the path were caves, dug into the sandy rock which covered the countryside. One cave especially attracted her attention. It seemed to cast a blinding light onto the path.

A great star hovered over it, almost touching the roof. Lady Pride drew closer, pausing now and then as if afraid to get too close.

The wooden door of the cave was full of chinks and holes. It was just an old stable door. The cave was used, it seemed, only to house animals. Lady Pride was, for once, unsure of herself and strangely troubled. Then, slowly, she opened the door, not really expecting to see anyone.

On the contrary, she saw a woman holding a Child in her arms. There was a man kneeling in seeming adoration. The man made a step or two toward the door, as if to bar the way. The woman shook her head gently, and the man stopped.

Lady Pride entered and gently closed the door behind her. The woman, a mere child herself, seemed to grow taller and more mature as she held up the Child and sang this song of praise: "My soul praises the Lord; my soul is glad because of God my Savior. For he has remembered me, his lowly servant! And from now on all people will call me blessed. . . ."

Lady Pride fell on her knees. Suddenly she knew that *this was the sight God had shown the angels* on the day she was born. She had not seen it then. She had only seen the frown of Lucifer, the Prince of Pride. It was this Child she had counseled him not to serve.

With her head in the straw which littered the floor, Lady Pride wept. She wept bitter, scalding tears of sorrow and compunction. She wished she were dead. She wished she had never been born. She wished she had never seen Lucifer or spoken to him. The enormity of her offense stood out so clearly that she was blinded by the sight.

But the Lady with the Child was smiling again. And, though Lady Pride did not hear any words spoken, she knew that she had been forgiven, and that henceforth she would never be the same. She had beheld with her own eyes the fullness of *Truth incarnate,* God made flesh, God and his Mother!

And that is how Lady Pride became humble. Today she takes pride only in the works of God, especially those wonders of grace he accomplishes in the hearts of men.

Lucifer wept too—but with anger. He picked up Haughtiness which Lady Pride had left on the straw of the cave and made it his own.

Thus it is that today, when men see a cold and haughty

beauty walking the earth, one who puts on a great arrogance and an insufferable pride, they see a ghostly reflection of the heart of Lucifer, the Angel of Light who became the Prince of Darkness.

How Lady Prudence
Became Gloriously Imprudent

In her own way, Lady Prudence was quite beautiful.
But it was her serious expressions, her deep concentration,
her slowness to come to any decision before she had exam-
ined every possible angle—these things made her look drab
and old. No man living could really tell her age, nor did
history remember when she started walking the earth. It just
seemed that she had always been here.

Lady Prudence really belonged to the retinue of Lady
Wisdom. Strange as this may seem, Lady Wisdom always
asked for the advice of Lady Prudence (even if it was a long
time forthcoming!), but she didn't always follow it. It was
noticed that, if and when Lady Prudence lingered alone and
decided to travel with this man or that, that man suddenly
became fearful, overcautious and began to take the longest
time coming to any decision. When he finally did come to
a decision, his choice was always austere, cold and lifeless.
Other men, while admiring the prudence of these decisions,
somehow felt uncomfortable about them. They sensed somehow that something was missing from these models of lucidity.
What was missing was anybody's guess.

Centuries came and centuries went. Each year became
acquainted with the slow, measured step of Lady Prudence.
If Time, catching sight of her cold and serious face, tried to
make her smile a little, he never succeeded.

One day Lady Prudence was walking through Palestine.
In one small village she was attracted to a certain house be-

cause of a blinding light that seemed to envelop it. She looked through the window and saw a young woman sitting on an old-fashioned chair. At her feet was an angel. The girl was speaking softly but quite clearly, telling the angel that, though she was a virgin, she was also the handmaid of God, and was ready to do whatever God wanted her to do.

For once in her life Lady Prudence was deeply moved. And, would you believe it, a smile almost started on her lips! But then she caught herself, frowned, became serious and business-like again. She shook her head in dismay. All this talk was highly imprudent! What a scandal it would create! What of the girl's husband? There should be much more thought given by that lovely girl to what the angel was asking.

Still shaking her head Lady Prudence walked away, muttering and wondering to herself. And, though she traveled in many countries, Palestine kept attracting her. In a few years she was back there again, walking its dusty roads, seeking she knew not what or whom. Maybe that extraordinary woman-child had been imprudent in a holy way!

Was she looking for her? If so she did not find her. She came to a well in Samaria. She saw there One who almost made her forget the girl. One look at his face and Prudence knew he was an extraordinary man. Having been so long in the retinue of Wisdom, and being a bit wise in her own right, Prudence thought for just a moment that surely this wonderful stranger was more than just a man.

Just then a Samaritan woman came to the well. The Man, unmistakably a Jew, seemed to know all about her. He was aware that she was a "loose woman." In the course of the conversation it came out that she had had five husbands! Nevertheless, he was drinking out of her water jar and telling her most extraordinary things about God. Most imprudent, Lady Prudence thought! Truly scandalous! She turned abruptly and walked in the direction of the hills.

That night she was deeply disturbed. She worked hard

at the two puzzles of the young woman and this Man (for somehow they seemed connected). She wrestled with them way into the wee hours of the morning. Then, unable to come to any conclusion—a rare thing for her!—she went back and found the Man. She began to follow him wherever he went.

One day she heard him talk about the poor, the meek and the pure of heart. She actually heard him say that "those who would lose their lives would save them." It all seemed so imprudent! She left again, and allowed many days to pass before she would seek him out once more.

She watched him eat with Publicans. She saw him allow another "loose woman" to kiss his feet and anoint them with perfume. Again and again she was both puzzled and angry at his imprudent ways. She longed to stop him, have a good talk with him, point out to him how much and how often he was lacking in prudence. But somehow she couldn't find the courage to do so.

Exasperated, she shook the dust of Palestine off her sandals and went away. But—it was no use. She just had to see him again.

This time she met him in a narrow, cobbled street. His face was swollen and bloody. He was stumbling and falling under the weight of an enormous cross. She saw another man pulled from the crowd and forced to help him carry it.

It was at that moment that an unusual thing happened to Lady Prudence. Throwing caution to the wind (!) she made her way through the crowd, stumbling and tripping in her haste. She grabbed his cross and lifted it so high that it was now barely touching his bleeding shoulders. (No one, of course, saw her do it; everyone thought it was the man.)

But the Man knew. Together, Incarnate Love and Lady Prudence walked to the holy hill. There she met again the young woman, his mother. With her and Mary of Magdala, Lady Prudence kept the long and tragic vigil. She stayed until the end, saw the tomb sealed, then walked away with the others.

Wisdom was the first to notice the change. Lady Prudence was no longer the cold, serious Lady everyone knew. From that day on, Lady Wisdom always listened very carefully to what Prudence had to say. She seemed to have acquired a sort of "holy imprudence" which was that "something missing" in her character. She smiled more often too! And everyone knows now that holy Prudence seems awfully imprudent to men at times. But, oh, how pleasing it is to God!

How Humility Grew
Into Simplicity

Princess Humility was lovely. She knew it, and rendered glory to God for her beauty. Being born of Truth, she never attributed to herself anything that belonged to anyone else, especially God. She was meticulous, in fact, almost tediously so, in rendering what was due and where it was due and to whom it was due.

She was very slender. Some might have called her too thin. Her eyes were the color of violets in the spring. They were fresh and dewy, with long lashes. They seemed always to be working overtime, veiling the beautiful eyes. Man often wondered how Princess Humility could really see at all, walking all the time as she did with downcast eyes. But she *could* see, and very well too. Men, of course, do not know everything. They were unaware of the deep insights that guided the Princess on her constant journeyings.

Her hair was a warm brown, tightly braided and wound in a coronet on her well-shaped head. Now and then it had copper glints that made a strange, uneven halo. Of this she was not aware. Much of her time was spent thinking, analyzing and trying to figure things out. She had much to do, for it was her duty to impart her clear knowledge of values, and even her strange and lovely fragrance, to men's minds and hearts.

She was born with the dawn of Time. She only remembered that far back. Her mother, Queen Truth, had told her that, before Time, there was a timelessness called Eternity.

Life then had been beautiful. But a tragedy had happened to two very nice people called Adam and Eve. They had disobeyed God, and he had had to punish them.

Thus Death was born. Thus Time had to come forth to measure Life, and, at certain moments, hand it over to Death. Of course, Death died too, that is to say, she had become Life also. But "that is another story," Truth had said to her daughter, "which I will tell you sometime."

Princess Humility wished that she could hear that story soon, for it seemed a very interesting story from what little she knew of it. However, stories could wait. She had work to do, and hard work at that. For every time she moved in to live with men, they resented her coming.

In spite of her gentleness and beauty, they seemed to dislike her. Her fragrance did not appeal to them. Her razor-sharp knowledge, which opened their eyes to the immensity of Truth and to their utter dependence on a Power greater than they, hurt them. They would push her out of their homes and lock their doors to all her loveliness. They seemed to prefer her most powerful enemy—Lady Pride.

Some who accepted her became intensely happy. Order entered their lives. Happiness and Order were fragrant with Humility's fragrance, and men, in spite of themselves, respected those who walked with her.

Still, Princess Humility felt that, in some strange way, she lacked something herself. This life of constant analysis of motives and actions, this need to constantly remember she was nothing and that God was everything—all this was wearing her down.

She was becoming thinner still, ethereal, almost ghostlike. But she never faltered. She would delve deeper and deeper into her nothingness, other people's goodness and God's majesty. She spent much time trying to pass on to men her findings, such as men would listen to.

One day she was passing through a small village called

Nazareth. She was a little on the weary side. As it was a sunny and glorious day, she thought she would rest in the green meadow dotted with big yellow buttercups.

She was almost falling asleep when suddenly it seemed to her that one of the buttercups was bigger than all the buttercups she had ever seen in her whole long life. She sat up and rubbed her violet eyes, and then smiled. It wasn't a buttercup at all. It was the fair-haired head of a beautiful Child, a boy about four or five years old. He must have been lying down in the flowers. He stood up straight and smiled at her.

Humility smiled back. The Child walked to her and invited her to play ball with him. It was a wooden ball (rubber being unknown at the time). It was painted a vivid, regal red. The Princess hesitated. She looked at herself, examining all her motives and intentions as was her custom. She found herself still lacking some things she could not define. She yearned to rush up to the Child and play ball with him, but something held her back.

She thought of her whole life. She always knew there was room for improvement. She thought of her nothingness and of her unimportance. Could it be that *what she was, Humility,* kept her from playing with the Child?

The Child, cocking his head to one side, surveyed her thoroughly. Then, speaking quite distinctly, told her that she needed to grow. She was all right most of the time, he said, but she should not stop growing. Her "growth" should be downward, into littleness. He sang a song to her:

Come on   And then
Get small   You will
Come and   Grow very big
Play ball   My dear Humility.
With me.

Because you will
Meet Simplicity
And she will
Teach you
How to be
A child like me.
And then
You will
Understand
That it is
Not enough
To know
Your nothingness
But that to
Grow and grow
With me

You have
To be
Simplicity
And then
You will be
All filled
With Charity.
Come, play ball
With me.
I am Simplicity;
And I will
Teach you
How to be
As simple
As me!

Something happened to Princess Humility. She ran and played ball with the Child all afternoon. Then, at sunset, when she threw the ball back to him for the last time, he seemed to vanish. So did the ball. Both he and the ball blended into the sunset.

From that day to this, Princess Humility teaches men that she is but the handmaid of Simplicity.

How Ugly Lady Pain Became So Beautiful

From the dawn of time there lived among men a strange and austere woman. She was tall and thin, and few knew the color of her eyes. Whenever people looked into her eyes they seemed to change from light blue or grey into hopeless and lusterless black or deep violet.

Her face was filled with lines, ugly, ugly with all the ugliness to be seen in the world. Her only true claim to beauty was her raven black hair. This too was seldom seen because she wore strange, floating, grey garments which merged with the darkness that followed her everywhere; it accompanied her arrival whenever men could see her.

But few ever had any desire to behold her for long. They did all they could to give her a wide berth. If she moved in on them, or stopped to look at them, they besought all the gods they knew to remove her from them. For wherever she went she brought pain—searing, tearing, gnawing pain— that drove men mad or sent them to an early grave.

Few escaped her. At one time or another, in every man's life, she would come to visit him. She would bend down and, taking the person in her arms, hold him tight. When he was quite dead she would let him go. Yes, she was queen of an immense domain, ugly Lady Pain.

One moonlit night she found herself in a garden of olive trees. She loved the gnarled and strange shapes etched against the brilliant night. From afar, she saw a Man kneeling before a stone. He seemed to be in utter exhaustion. She moved closer. The Man's face, lifted to heaven, became distorted by an inner pain which she was conscious was not of her own making. Intrigued, she advanced still nearer. Beads of blood were trickling down the ghostly white face.

Suddenly, he saw her. An angel, all light, was at the moment holding out a shining chalice to his lips. Over the rim the Man smiled at Lady Pain. No one had ever smiled at her before! She paused to think this over.

At that moment a large crowd came into the garden. There was a great deal of noise and commotion. A man stepped from the crowd and kissed the One who had drunk from the shining chalice. Then he was led away.

Lady Pain followed; she could not help herself. She really did not want to go, but somehow she had to. For the first time in her whole existence a force greater than her own compelled her. She gradually lost sight of him. Her heart beat wildly over her loss. She could not rest now. She had to find the Man who had smiled upon her.

In the distance she heard the all too familiar sounds of floggings. She had always attended such affairs; otherwise there would be nothing to them. Although she felt strangely reluctant, she went anyway.

And there he was, being flogged by the Roman soldiers. She could not comprehend what was happening to her. She wanted to cry out, to stop the torture, to put her thin body between him and the whips. But she could not move. For an instant he lifted his head. Again their eyes met, and he smiled.

She covered her face with her thin, gaunt hands and wept. The feeling of tears was utterly new to her. She pondered over that. Later, when she saw him mocked and crowned with thorns, anger took hold of her. But before she could move against his enemies with her own deadly power, they took him inside the palace.

Disconsolate, unable to bear the pain that had flooded

her heart so suddenly, the queen of pain walked away. She was majestic even in her grief. Whoever met her in this condition took one look at her and ran as if his very life depended on it.

Day passed into night. She found herself on a hill on which three crosses stood. On the cross in the middle hung the Man, crucified. He hung there like a piece of fruit dying on a branch. She could not endure the pain which came to her from that dying figure. She ran up to the very foot of the cross. She started to tear the heavy nails from his feet. Blood, his blood, fell on her and coursed gently down her face and garments.

She looked up and saw that he was dead. She looked at her clothes and noticed that they had been dyed ruby red. She turned, and a wave of admiration rippled through the onlooking crowd. Slowly she walked away. She sat down by the side of a lake to rest. She saw her face reflected on the calm surface of the water. She did not like to see herself most of the time. But—what was this? She did not recognize herself! She was beautiful! Somehow her eyes had been purified and she saw beyond her ugliness to her beauty within.

And that is why ever since men who are able to see more deeply know that Love wedded himself to Lady Pain, and that Love can make her beautiful—as beautiful as she saw herself on that day of Love's death.